KILL HOLE

KILL HOLE

JAMAKE HIGHWATER

GROVE PRESS

NEW YORK

▲

At the close of the twentieth century there are many voices that echo in our blood memory: writers, composers, and poets whose creations resonate in our lives and in our imaginations. Kill Hole is imbued with traces of that blood memory. It is a tribute to the artists who have shaped both my life and my work.

▼

Published by Grove Press
A division of Grove Press, Inc.
841 Broadway
New York, NY 10003-4793

Published in Canada by General Publishing Company, Ltd.

Library of Congress Cataloging-in-Publication Data

Highwater, Jamake.
    Kill hole / Jamake Highwater—1st ed.
        p.   cm.
    ISBN 0-8021-1475-X (acid-free paper)
    I. Title.
    PS3558.I373K5   1992
    813'.54—dc20   92-14492
                                                CIP

Manufactured in the United States of America

Printed on acid-free paper

Designed by Marie-Helene Fredericks

First Edition 1992

10   9   8   7   6   5   4   3   2   1

For COLEEN CHERICI

▲

When asked the familar question, "If your house were on fire and you could take away only one thing, what would it be?" Jean Cocteau answered: "J'emporterais le feu"—

I would take the fire.

▼

PART I: DEPARTURE

"LOOKING BACK"

*It seemed to him the pale and lovely Summoner out there
smiled at him and beckoned; as though, with the hand he
lifted from his hip, he pointed outward as he hovered above
an immensity of richest expectation. And, as so often before,
he rose to follow.*

—THOMAS MANN, *Death in Venice*

O N E

I have seen so many things fall I once believed were
eternal.

—STENDHAL

SOMEONE MUST HAVE been telling lies about Sitko Ghost
Horse, because without having done anything wrong he was
arrested. It was on the Night of the Washing of the Hair that
he became a prisoner.

A breeze sprang up suddenly, coming down cold, damp,
and with the odor of burning grass. The sweet stench of the
smoke drifted through his mind, reminding him of the embrace of his grandmother Amana. The memory of her strong
eyes distracted him from the the pain in his wrists as his
captors bound his hands behind him.

It was in the night of burning grass that Sitko was arrested.
The Two Horn Priests fell upon him and would not go away.

"What are you doing here?" they whispered. "Who are
your people? Are you evil or are you good?"

Sitko insisted upon his innocence, but they would not
release him.

He struggled against the ropes that restrained him. He fell
to the ground and clung to the underbrush as they dragged

3

him through the smoldering grassland. He fought against them until he fainted from pain. Even in his dreams he tried to escape from them. And when he recovered his senses, he pleaded with them to let him go. He cried out for help. He shouted and screamed. So they filled his mouth with ashes. Still he gestured frantically into the emptiness of the land, searching for someone who would defend him. But nothing he did and nothing he said would make the Two Horn Priests go away.

It was in that long-ago Night of the Washing of the Hair that Sitko changed into a prisoner.

Looking back, he saw the hills enveloped in a dense white fog. The world vanished into the vapor that tumbled down upon them. Blood froze on his wrists. The night gradually filled with inconsolable cries. Ten thousand tortured cats. A piercing whine conveying an everlasting, inexpressible misery. Then the sky turned to silver dust that swirled upward in the wind.

"*Oo-ke!* . . . Let's go," the Two Horn Priests shouted over the gale, pushing their prisoner toward their encampment.

By the time they descended into the circle of smoky adobe houses, piled one on top of the other, the fog had changed into sleet. A vicious Moon crept into the sky and peered down upon Sitko's misery, smiling her silver smile and playing her dark music as she vanished behind a cloud.

In the dark of the Moon, Sitko saw them for the first time. The gray people, whose wet, naked bodies gleamed like newly modeled vessels of clay. They made their way cautiously into the bonfire's yellow light, covering their eyes, blinded by the blaze. Their motley whiskers hung about their faces and their round ears quivered nervously as they gazed at

4

Sitko, astonished and curious, sniffing the air for traces of him.

He shivered and opened his mouth without speaking.

"Who are you?" one of the Two Horn Priests demanded in a whisper. "Why are you here? Are you good or are you evil? What is it that we see in your eyes?"

It was in this night of the dark Moon that Sitko Ghost Horse began the fight for his life.

TWO

▲

SHE DID NOT look at him. She silently placed his food upon a ledge. Then she hobbled slowly along the gray walls of the small chamber, dragging her withered leg behind her. She muttered to herself. Words he could not understand. She shook her head and sighed. Then she leaned heavily against a corner of the room and carefully lowered her massive body to the floor.

She turned her head to the side. And then, without the slightest interest or anger, she stared at him. As a wolf looks at a rabbit.

Finally, she snorted with indifference and turned away.

Now it was silent. Sitko could hear nothing but his own breathing, as if he were the only survivor in the world.

The light faded from the little window in the room. With the darkening of the sky the silence was broken by the drone of evening. Insects began their desperate drumming. From everywhere came the piping of tree frogs. An airplane made its way so high above the village that its roar was a fragile sigh.

Sitko Ghost Horse ate without appetite, without knowing or wondering what he was eating. Then he tried to stand on his bruised feet. Pain pulsed through his legs, and he became dizzy and fell against the wall, turning breathless and pallid. He was tempted to slide back to the ground, but he refused to relent to the pain. That was something his grandmother had taught him. "I hope you are not feeling sorry for yourself," she would say to him. "You must learn to use the pain to rise above whatever it is that harms you."

Gradually he straightened his back and took a faltering breath as he made his way to the window. He was astonished by the blackness of the world outside. There had never been quite such a night as this. As he pressed his face against the bars, the sky taught him something about darkness that he had never known. And about stars. Towering above his prison was the endless trail of the sky, twisting outward through the vast and glittering beadwork of stars. He trembled from the cold, or perhaps from the immensity of the night, feeling utterly powerless and alone.

"How long have I been here?" he whispered to the woman, who had come out of her dark corner and was eagerly eating the food he had left in his bowl.

She did not answer.

"How long have I been here and what do they want from me?"

She looked up from the bowl and blinked at him. Then her lips curled slightly as she grinned, and she rubbed the back of her large hand against her chin.

Her expression angered him. "I hope you know that you can get in trouble for doing this to me."

Still she said nothing.

7

Her indifference began to frighten him. "I hope you know that it's not right to keep me here against my will."

She ran her fingers along the inside of the bowl and licked them without taking her eyes from him. Then she silently collected his dish and hobbled to the door and pounded on it. Sitko heard the bolt move. Lantern light flooded into the room, and a Two Horn Priest stood in the doorway.

"Wait!" Sitko exclaimed, as the woman was leaving.

She turned to him momentarily, a large tin can in her hand. Again she grinned as she dropped the can to the ground. "For you," she said in a deep, masculine voice. "Piss in this. Shit in this. My name is Patu. I will come back."

The door slammed shut behind her. And Sitko Ghost Horse was alone in the dark.

THREE

▲

"I MAKE PICTURES," Sitko Ghost Horse said, watching the woman's eyes for a sign of comprehension. "I'm a painter. Do you know? A painter. . . ."

She looked at him doubtfully with the trace of a grin, as if she might be thinking that he was a liar or a fool.

"It is true . . . a painter . . . I'm a painter," he insisted, as he snatched a charred stick from the tiny fire that warmed the room and began to outline the image of a large woman on the adobe wall.

The woman watched with little interest, until her likeness began to appear upon the gray surface. A towering figure, with broad shoulders and a large chest. A square face with a strong jaw and a full mouth.

Her image took shape so quickly that it seemed to seep from the adobe itself rather than being the creation of Sitko's rapidly moving fingers.

"No!" the woman exclaimed as her face began to appear upon the wall, as even the expression of panic in her eyes was

9

captured in the eyes of the woman taking shape before her. "No, no, no!" she shouted, staggering forward and trying to brush her image from the wall. "Let me go! Let me off the wall!" she pleaded. "I am not the prisoner! You are the prisoner! You must let me go!"

Sitko was astonished by the woman's strength as she forced her way past him and frantically rubbed away the lines he had drawn, until, at last, the figure had become a clouded ghost smeared across the gray adobe.

"Then you must tell me," Sitko whispered, coming close to the woman and grasping her large hand. "You must tell me why I am a prisoner."

She looked at him in fear and anger, pulling her hand away, and peering first at the wall and then at Sitko.

"That is why . . ." she murmured under her breath, as if she were speaking the unspeakable. "*That* is why."

"But I don't understand," he insisted, following after her as she retreated toward the door. "And I must be able to understand. Don't you see? I have to understand why you are keeping me here."

She was terrified. She shook her head and mumbled something again and again. She thrust out her hands and made a sign in the air, as if it would protect her from him.

"All right . . . all right . . ." he murmured, as he backed away slowly, trying to calm her by raising his hands in a placating gesture.

"If I promise," he pleaded, "if I promise not to make any more pictures of you, will you tell me? Will you tell me why I am here?"

"No, no, no," she muttered, swinging around and pounding on the door. "No!"

Instantly the door swung open and a priest stepped into the room. He automatically raised his arm, and in his hand he held a long, thin, double-edged knife.

Sitko fell back.

The woman rushed behind the priest. Then she turned to face Sitko, and in a hoarse voice full of fear and rage she whispered, "You are a prisoner. You are a prisoner because you do evil. That is why you are a prisoner. You are a prisoner because only evil can cross the barriers of pollen and come here and put a curse on the children. That is why you are a prisoner. That is why. . . ."

The door closed slowly, and Sitko Ghost Horse stared at the misty image of the woman on the wall, trying to understand the meaning of her words. Trying to fathom the things she had told him. What was the evil she feared? How could pollen make a barrier? It didn't make any sense. What curse and what evil and what children?

Feeling utterly hopeless, Sitko looked into the sky beyond the little window. He watched as a star darted across the black heavens and died in the mouth of darkness at the edges of the world. He leaned against the wall, overwhelmed by exhaustion and confusion. He knew he had to get control of himself. He needed to rest. He needed to sleep. He needed to stop thinking. *Somehow he had to stop thinking!*

Sinking to the floor, he curled up and wrapped his arms around his chest, squeezing his eyes tightly closed and trying to sleep. But each time his mind slipped beyond his control, confusion overtook him, becoming a violent storm of fear that rumbled through his body.

What would they do to him? Why did they hate him? What had he done?

Sleep . . . try to sleep.
No!
Think . . . try to think.

He had frightened her. That much he understood. It was a stupid mistake to have drawn a likeness of her. He realized that at once. But what about the rest of it? What did it mean?

Again and again he asked himself the same questions.

Whatdidshemeanbybarriersofpollenhowcouldyouusepollentomake abarrieritdidn'tmakeanysensewhatcurseandwhatevilandwhatyoung ones?

The walls began to splinter and crumble, turning into gray dust. The dust billowed upward and changed into a talking cloud. *Talking talking talking.* He listened to the words, but they made no sense. He stared into the talking cloud, but it began to disappear. He groaned softly as he gazed helplessly into the whirlwind, where he saw himself streak across an immense sky and plummet into the mouth of darkness that opened wide at the edges of the world.

F O U R

Sitko Ghost Horse could hear someone moaning.

"Eric?" he called out. "Is that you, Eric?"

The muffled sounds of someone moaning awakened him. Even before opening his eyes, he automatically reached out to comfort his friend. But Eric was not there.

Sitko leaped to his feet and stared into the moonlight. Slowly he realized that he was far from home, in a little room where he was a prisoner.

At once a frantic feeling overran his mind. He groaned as he staggered into consciousness, rising from a troubled sleep and fleeing the lingering shadows of a dreadful dream. *A dead man.* It was the dream of a dead man. *A world of dead men.* It was a dream about a world filled with dead men.

"Eric? Is that you, Eric?"

No. Of course not. It could not be Eric. He was gone.

Sitko pressed his fingers to his forehead, trying to snatch the nightmare from his brain. Trying to emerge from sleep. Only then did he begin to recognize the gray walls and stout

13

wooden door of his prison. Instantly, with that recognition, the pain returned to his legs, and he sank back to the earthen floor where he had slept, panting senselessly.

He had to collect himself. That much he knew. If he was to survive he had to think carefully about what was happening to him.

He took a deep breath and sat up, determined to concentrate on nothing but the events that had brought him here.

He had fled. He remembered his desperation as he had fled from the sickness, leaving the city with nothing but the memory of death. He had driven for perhaps two days and nights until he could no longer remain conscious. It had been evening when he abandoned his automobile and started aimlessly across the wasteland, with no notion of where he was or where he was going. His only thought had been to keep moving so he could not think about what had happened to him.

He had walked for a very long time before hearing the distant sound of drumming and chanting. Only then had he seen the trace of smoke rising from a little cluster of earthen houses tucked among piñon pines and flowering datura. Then, suddenly, as he had entered the village, he had been seized. For no reason he had been captured by strangers and thrown into this room. That was all he could remember, until he had awakened to the sound of someone sobbing.

"Eric? Is that you, Eric?"

Looking back, Sitko could see sunshine flooding through the windows of a large white room. He could hear the rattle of a typewriter. Eric was working. Eric was always working, hunched over his desk in their large white room.

Looking back, he could see Eric smiling. He could see his

long lean body slowing turning toward him. He could hear his laughter. He could see him at the summit of a hill. He could see him at the dinner table. Laughing.

"Eric? Is that you, Eric?" he cried out.

There was no answer.

He limped to the window. He could still hear the distant sound of weeping. Beyond the window, somewhere in the darkness of the village, there was the sound of children crying.

Looking back into the shifting moonlight, he could see a child among the trees. He could see a boy with tears in his brown eyes. Looking back through the glimmer of moonlight, he could see his mother leading him away. It had been in the evening, when the birds were still singing, that his mother had led him away from the house of Grandma Amana.

The old woman knelt in front of Sitko and embraced him with such intensity that it hurt his shoulders. Then she covered her face and turned away from the child as his mother pulled him along after her, out into an evening so vast and empty that he began to cry.

Even now he could still hear the sound of that long-ago child. Beyond the window, somewhere in the darkness, there was the sound of a little boy weeping.

Sitko had been too young to understand what was happening to him, but the grief of his grandmother and the panic on his mother's face had made him feel that something terrible was taking place. A great stone began to burn in his belly. He could no longer hear the song of the birds, but only the fierce cry tumbling from his own mouth.

It was Saturday. It was a rainy Saturday. He stood dumbfounded, staring at the children who ran up and down the hallway, while his mother talked quietly to the lady seated at the desk, answering her questions self-consciously.

"Sitko," his mother said. "His name is Sitko Ghost Horse. He has one older brother named Reno. . . . Yes, that's right, Reno . . . like in Nevada."

The lady wrote everything down on a long yellow paper. The rapid motion of the woman's pen worried Sitko's mother, and she tilted her head to the side in an effort to read what the lady was writing. "I really wanted to keep Sitko at home, but his father . . ."

"What about his father?" the woman interrupted. "What became of the father? What's the father's background?"

"Some kind of Indian. . . . I think he's Cherokee."

The woman looked up with an expression of impatience. "You think?"

"He's Cherokee," Sitko's mother repeated nervously. "He's definitely Cherokee. And, well, he just went off . . . about four months ago. And we haven't heard a word from him. Not a word. And we just can't manage on our own. Not without Jamie. That's my husband. Jamie Ghost Horse. . . ."

"And you . . . what kind of Indian are you?"

"Me?"

"Yes, you. Are you also of Indian heritage?"

"Why no," Sitko's mother lied, sounding as if she were astonished by the question. "I'm French. I'm French Canadian. My maiden name was Bonneville. Jemina Bonneville."

Looking back, Sitko could see his mother. On a rainy Saturday. The empty sky was filled with gray rain, and in his belly was a stone. That is all he could remember. The burning in his stomach. The rain. And the forlorn eyes of all the

16

children who gathered in the doorway and peered at him, until the woman at the desk sent them away with an angry gesture.

Everything he had ever feared was happening. To be lost in the dark. To be alone in a place from which he could not escape.

He grasped his mother's hand fiercely, sensing that at any moment she would leave him. He tried to believe that his mother would not do such a thing to him. But the stone turned slowly in his belly, and it burned.

Jemina Bonneville stood up abruptly. Then, without looking back at Sitko, she fled from the room.

He shouted after her. He wheeled around as the woman caught him in her firm grasp. She was smiling, but her fingers hurt his arms. "I bet your name is Sitko," she was saying in a sweet voice. "Is that what your name is?"

He could not free himself from her grip. He stared into her pale face and tried desperately not to cry.

"Don't you want to tell me your name?"

He leaned away from her, afraid he was going to be sick.

"Such a big fellow . . . you're not going to cry, now, are you," she said as she pulled him down the immense hallways where the children stopped and stared and whispered.

He searched the doorways for his mother, but she was gone. He clenched his teeth each time he felt tears coming into his eyes. But he could not stop the burning stone that was slowly rising in his chest. He could not stop the fear that filled his throat. And then he began to groan, for he realized he was urinating in his pants.

"Shame on you! Filthy boy!" the woman shouted, pushing him backward into a dark closet and slamming the door.

"You just stay in there, young man, until you learn how to behave!"

He pounded on the door. He shouted and begged to be let out. But no one answered his calls. He turned slowly around and around, trying to catch his breath, feeling urine running down his legs and into his shoes. His shouts collapsed in his chest as he was overwhelmed by a sense of helplessness. He cowered in an immense darkness, feeling more alone than he had ever felt in his life.

Now, once again, he was alone in a dark room. It was no longer Saturday. And the gray rain of that long-ago afternoon had ended. His mother was gone. Grandma Amana was gone. Eric was gone. Everyone he had ever loved was gone. And Sitko Ghost Horse stood silently in a little room and in the dark, watching the moonlight streaming through the window of his prison as it slowly crept across the wall where a misty woman stood in a cloud, and everywhere in the night he could hear the distant voices of children weeping.

Soon the pitiless Moon turned her back on him and hurried from the sky. He searched the corners of the dark room, seeing the faint white glimmer of owls. He whimpered and backed against the wall. And then he waited. He waited in silence for the monsters of the room to attack him. The stone turned slowly in his belly, and it burned.

F I V E

▲

THE TWO HORN Priests awakened Sitko Ghost Horse in the middle of the night. He was in a daze. All he could hear was the resonant clacking of the turtle-shell rattles bound to the priests' legs. He groaned, but they would not leave him in peace. They leaned over him, shaking him and shouting. Their stern faces were covered with white paint, and they wore crowns with long, floppy horns that reached high above their heads and jostled to and fro when they moved.

As the priests tied Sitko's hands behind his back, they argued with one another, disputing which of them had the greater authority in regard to the prisoner. They pushed him from one to another and shouted at each other. Finally, without resolving their quarrel, they led Sitko from his prison.

He had been confined to the dark little room for so long that the openness of the world made him a bit dizzy. The Moon glared into his eyes, taking keen delight in his degradation. But Sitko was so drained of dignity that he could not grasp the humiliation of his situation. And he was not sufficiently awake to think clearly.

For all he knew this was the end. Perhaps they had decided to kill him. Just to be done with it. Or perhaps they had decided to take him to the edge of the village and turn him loose. Somehow it didn't matter anymore. He didn't care where they were taking him. He followed blindly as they tugged upon the rope that was fastened to a collar around his neck.

Sitko staggered, feeling ill, and was barely able to remain on his feet.

"Wait," he pleaded, when he stumbled. "I must rest for a moment."

They ignored him and continued to drag him along without looking back.

Sitko panted desperately. He tried to catch his breath, but that made him feel worse. His lungs filled with the overwhelming stench of deadly datura blossoms carried by the night air. He sank to the ground in a faint, blinded by the dust.

"Let him rest!" he heard a familiar voice demand.

A trickle of water seeped between his dry lips, reviving him. A hand touched his head. A gentle touch like the hand of Grandmother Amana.

When he opened his eyes he saw the face of his grandmother, looking down at him with concern. Then, gradually, the face began to change; first into a luminous lantern, and then into a Halloween pumpkin. Finally it changed into the face of Patu.

She whispered to him, "Do not be afraid. It is all right. The

20

elders want to talk. They will ask many things. But it is all right."

There was a brief exchange between the Two Horn Priests and Patu, and, finally, they reluctantly handed her the rope.

"Come," she coaxed, "only a few steps and you will be there."

Sitko struggled to his feet and crept slowly forward, while the Two Horn Priests muttered with annoyance.

When he got to their destination, he felt as though he were entering a meeting hall. But the room where he was taken was underground and had to be entered by way of a ladder through a hole in the roof. A crowd filled the room, in which there was an upper level, like a gallery, just below the roof, also quite packed, where the people were able to stand only if they bent down, with their heads and backs touching the ceiling.

Feeling that the air was too thick for him, Sitko stepped back, but Patu said: "Go inside."

Sitko might not have obeyed if she had not come up to him, grasped the hatchway door, and said: "I must shut this door after you. Nobody else must come in."

So he took a deep breath and then climbed down the ladder into the crowded subterranean room.

A hand reached out and seized him. It belonged to a dwarf with a large, bald head that was covered with soft mud oozing slowly over his face.

"Come along, come along," the dwarf said.

Sitko let himself be led off. It seemed that in the confused, swarming crowd a small path was kept open, possibly separating two different clans or factions of the village. The people on his left were talking loudly, while those standing on his right were silent. Why they were assembled in two groups he did not know, but it seemed apparent that they were there to debate Sitko's fate. Yet, as he was ushered to a raised area at one end of the chamber, these people showed not the slightest interest in Sitko.

When they reached the platform, the dwarf removed the rope from Sitko's neck, but he did not speak. Instead he made a series of highly exaggerated gestures. Sitko could not understand what the dwarf was trying to convey to him. This confusion brought a roar of amusement from the noisy people standing on the left. The dwarf was both delighted and annoyed with Sitko's failure to understand him. His little stump of a body seemed to go into spasms, as his gestures became frantic. As a result, the laughter in the chamber grew deafening. Sitko tried again and again to grasp the meaning of the dwarf's manic pantomime, until, at last, he understood that the dwarf wanted him to climb on top of the little platform and stand on it, in a position just above the heads of the surrounding crowd.

The stuffiness of the airless chamber worsened Sitko's dizziness, and it was only with the greatest effort that he managed to obey the instructions, climbing onto the tiny ledge and balancing there. Then, suddenly, there was a brief barrage of drumming, followed by a distant voice rising from a low chant to a wild outcry. At this moment the woman named Patu stood up in the midst of the silent people on Sitko's right. At the same time, an old man took his place at the head of the noisy crowd on the left.

Without any introduction, the man said: "Well, then, you are a housepainter?"

"No," Sitko replied without hesitation. "I am an artist. I paint pictures."

This response provoked such an outburst of infectious laughter from the people on the left that Sitko, despite his confusion and humiliation, found that even he began to laugh. The room reeled with laughter.

Meanwhile the people in the right half of the chamber remained completely silent. They stood calmly in rows, gazing at Sitko without the slightest expression on their faces. Without exception, these silent people were very old men. Sitko studied their vacant faces. Could they be the influential men of the village, men whose opinion could sway everyone else? Was it they who would determine his fate? And if so, what could he say to them to win their sympathy? How might he defend himself?

"What have I done?" Sitko cried out, in a voice so loud that the laughter instantly ceased, and everyone in the chamber fell silent. "Why have you made me a prisoner? Why have you locked me up and tied my hands? And what have I done to deserve such treatment?"

The silence lasted only a moment, for Sitko's emotional outburst produced even greater laughter than before. The people on the left mocked his words by trying to repeat them to one another.

The man standing in the crowd ignored the upheaval, and in an imposing voice he demanded: "Who are you?"

"My name is Sitko Ghost Horse."

"What does that mean?" the man asked with a belittling tone of voice. At this the laughter of the crowd grew so loud that Sitko could barely hear the questions asked of him.

"Where do you come from? Who are your people?"

"My name is Sitko Ghost Horse!" Sitko repeated in a shout. "My name is Sitko Ghost Horse! But I don't know where I come from. I don't know where or when I was born!"

"Why do you not know such things?"

"Because . . . because I was taken away from my people when I was a little boy! That is why!"

"Can you prove who you are?"

"How can I prove such a thing? How can anybody prove such a thing?"

"Where do you come from? Who are your people?" the man repeated in a much louder voice.

"My grandmother was called Amana! Her husband was Far Away Son! But he died. She had a child. With a stranger. That child was my mother, Jemina Bonneville! And my father was called Jamie Ghost Horse! And my foster father was named Alexander Milas-Miller. And when I was adopted I was called Seymour Miller. They called me Sy Miller. But I am Sitko Ghost Horse! That is who I am!"

The man smiled unpleasantly and remarked to the crowd: "He does not seem to know who he is."

"You must believe me!" Sitko shouted over the laughter. "My grandmother was called Amana! Her husband was Far Away Son! My mother was Jemina Bonneville! And my father was Jamie Ghost Horse! My brother was Reno! Those were my people! They are gone! Now all of them are gone! But they were my people!"

The man waved Sitko aside with a gesture of contempt. At this there was another burst of laughter. And then the man turned his back on Sitko, saying: "Take him away. He lies. He is not Sitko Ghost Horse. There is no such person. Take him away. He is something unclean and unnatural. He is something evil!" It seemed to give him intense pleasure to humiliate the prisoner. "He has brought filth to our village," he hissed with an awkward sweeping gesture of his flabby arms. And then he placed his narrow hands on his bulbous belly, whispering in a menacing voice: "He has poisoned the spirits of our children. Take him away!"

Now the upheaval of the crowd was deafening. The noise pounded in Sitko's head as he tried to find his breath in the stifling air of the chamber. He took a deep breath and fearfully backed away from the darkness that began to surround him. But he could not keep his balance. He lurched to one side and then to another, trying to stay on his feet. Then, suddenly, the hatch of the overhead door was thrown open, and his lungs were filled with the overwhelming stench of datura. He shouted. But no one could hear him. He slowly slipped into the air, tumbling into the black lake of the sky, where two million stars, one by one, closed their luminous eyes, leaving him alone in the dark.

He fell. And as he fell through that darkness he could smell the odor of burning grass, and he could hear the low, hissing babble of terrible accusations. And he could hear the distant sound of an airplane and everywhere the ferocious howl of inconsolable cries. Ten thousand tormented cats. A piercing whine conveying an everlasting and inexpressible misery. And the sky turned silver, and the Moon came out, smiling a dreadful, pallid smile. Silently she combed her long black hair, singing a little song to please herself. Then quite suddenly she turned upon him with a shout, and thrust her frigid fingers deep into his heart.

Moonlight exploded in his head, filling his mind with

25

silver splinters. Now, everywhere, the night was filled with the blinding dazzle of the Moon.

Looking back into the moonlight, Sitko could see a child alone among the eucalyptus trees. Looking back, he could see a boy standing over a ruined garden, with tears in his eyes. Looking back through the blaze of light, he could see his mother leading him away. Even now, he could still hear the desperate cry of that long-ago child. Beyond the world, somewhere in the darkness, there was still the inconsolable howl of that frightened child.

It was Sunday. The other children had gone away with their visitors. Now there was no one left but Sitko. As he wandered aimlessly among the trees that lined the little street, he could hear the whispers of the housemothers who watched from behind the blank, dark windows of the houses of the orphanage. He hurried away from their voices, which gradually faded into the babble of the fountain. The water moved so slowly that it had grown long, mossy beards upon the chins of the boy and girl who hovered under their umbrella in the fountain. He sat on the curb and imagined that he was a statue, safe and snug forever underneath a green umbrella. With pink cheeks and red lips and lovely soft blond hair. The droplets of water sang to him, ringing outward in a chorus of sighs. A few leaves drifted from the sky. A large yellow cat came to drink at the fountain, turning, as it swallowed, first into a leopard and then into a tiger. Its passionate roar sent all the housemothers fleeing from their windows. Sitko laughed with delight. But his voice startled the tiger, and it vanished without a trace.

The orphanage was called Star of Good Hope. Once or twice a week a mother came down the hallway, pulling along a boy or a girl. No matter where Sitko was at Star of Good Hope, he could always hear the weeping of the new children. And when he peeked into the office, he would see in the faces of the mothers the same torment that he had seen in his own mother's face. Then, before dark, the mothers would leave. Most of them never came back. Now the long hallways were empty. The children searched all the rooms for their parents. They called out in their sleep. But there were no mothers or fathers at the Star of Good Hope. There were just the housemothers and the schoolmaster and the men and women in uniforms. People without children of their own.

It was Sunday. Sitko sat on the curb in front of the big white dormitory building where he lived, watching for his mother or for Grandma Amana. But they did not come.

When it began to get dark and the other children returned from outings with their visiting relatives, Sitko was still sitting on the curb. He drew up his knees and buried his face in his hands, trying not to cry. He knew that he had been abandoned. He wanted to go to sleep until his life was over, until years and years of Sundays passed and all the parents had gone home and the sky turned dark forever. He wanted to sleep until he was no longer a child and could pack his things and leave Star of Good Hope, walking past the headmaster's house, down the lane that circled the little pine forest, past the church where they sang on Sunday mornings and past the fountain with its statue of a boy and girl standing beneath a bright green umbrella. He wanted to walk down the road that stretched beyond the painted line the children were not allowed to cross, through the gate at the road's end, where the railroad tracks ran into a long and distant sky.

It was on that Sunday of the fountain and the yellow cat

that Sitko Ghost Horse looked up and saw a familiar figure coming cautiously toward him. It was an older boy . . . a handsome fellow with pale blue eyes and a look of pride. He was gazing at Sitko as he approached, as though he were trying to understand his peculiar face, trying to figure out why this child was sitting alone by the fountain.

Sitko became apprehensive as the young man approached. Of all the people at Star of Good Hope whom Sitko had known, only this young man seemed to look at him. Sitko hoped they might become friends, for he had none at the orphanage. And this hope made Sitko all the more apprehensive, because it was so difficult for him to make friends.

The young man came still closer, and he looked down at Sitko as if he recognized him.

"What's your name?" he asked in a familiar voice, sitting on the curb beside Sitko and lightly touching his long black hair as if it amazed him.

Sitko was too shy to respond. He looked away self-consciously, for the familiar ring of the boy's voice touched him so deeply that it brought tears to his eyes.

"Do you live here?" he asked. "Or are you lost?"

"I live here, and I am lost," Sitko said.

Then the young man laughed joyously and embraced the little boy. "Sitko! Sitko! It's me . . . it's Reno, your brother!"

"No . . . no . . ." the child mumbled, weeping openly at the cruel joke of this young man. "My brother is gone. They took him away. I have no brother. He is gone."

"Look at this signet ring. It belonged to our father!" the young man exclaimed. "Then tell me if I am lying!"

Looking back into the moonlight, Sitko could not recall what happened next. The memory had turned into many colors, one upon the other. A deluge of yellow for their smiles, and green for the umbrella that shaded their reunion, and blue for the love Sitko saw in his brother's eyes.

It was on that Sunday of blue eyes and yellow tigers that Reno Ghost Horse came out of the shadows of the past to live at Star of Good Hope.

How beautiful he was! How everyone admired him! When he walked among the children, everyone smiled at him. His shirt was starched and his shoes were gleaming white.

Sitko watched his brother every night while he scrubbed his tennis shoes and bleached the laces. No one in the world had such clean sneakers. Everything that Reno did was wonderful. He was just sixteen, but already he was shaving. All his pimples had disappeared and his voice was handsome and low. When he sang and played his guitar, his voice was beautiful. And it didn't bother him in the least when the children came to listen to him sing. Nothing frightened Reno. The more people looked at him the stronger he became. His eyes glowed with power. When the children gazed at him in admiration, he opened up like a Chinese fan, with ever-widening beauty.

Sitko was fascinated and frightened by his brother's perfection. He loved to look at him, as long as Reno was unaware of his attention. He would stand at the window and watch him race around the baseball field while the other boys cheered. Sitko so greatly admired his brother that he was unable to speak to him unless spoken to first. Sitko loved and dreaded his attention. Standing next to his brother, Sitko felt small and worthless. He tried not to call attention to himself. So he did not speak. He withdrew into the shadows, where he could watch Reno without being noticed. And from that seclusion Sitko watched as Reno began to be transformed, like a cocoon, limb by limb, cell by cell, until he no longer existed. Until all at once, Reno became a butterfly!

Sometimes Sitko regretted that he could never become a butterfly. But he found joy in the realization that he could fly wherever he wanted to go on his brother's many-colored wings!

Sometimes Reno would read aloud. He insisted that Sitko watch carefully as he moved his finger along the mysterious marks that magically changed into words on his older brother's lips. Reno would pause in his reading and prompt Sitko to continue, but he did not understand how to turn the marks on the page into words. Sitko could not understand how even someone as smart as his brother could do something so remarkable: how he could change the marks on a page into marvelous stories!

Sitko loved the tales Reno read to him, but he could not easily recall the words. Words were not his friends. He was afraid that the stories would die if he did not remember them, and so he kept the stories alive inside of himself with a succession of bright images that flickered through his mind. He could summon these pictures at will, and when he was alone he often surrounded himself with them, basking in their brilliant colors and fantastic images. These pictures were Sitko's words and Sitko's stories. Pictures were his friends. And so he began to cover sheets of paper with images. And gradually he discovered how to bring life to the things that were hidden inside of him.

But these pictures did not interest the other children. When they looked at Sitko, they could not see inside of him, where his pictures lived. To them he would never be a butterfly. He was just a skinny little boy with long legs, funny hair, and a big nose.

So Sitko turned away from the playground, taking refuge behind the couch in the dormitory library, where he spent hours filling pages with the beauty hidden within him. He didn't know where the images came from, but foxes and owls and strange, unknown lands appeared in the pictures he drew—rising in smoke from the dark place in his heart where Grandma Amana's song and stories glowed luminous and blue.

Then one day the housemother told Sitko to go to the parlor. "There's someone here to see you," she said.

Sitko was frightened. No one had ever come to visit him. He grasped his brother's hand, afraid to leave him, but the housemother said, "Do as I say."

Reno pushed Sitko toward the door. Obediently, he slowly climbed the stairs, glancing back to make certain that Reno was following.

When they got to the top of the stairs, Sitko saw a tall, dark man standing in the doorway. He was holding a box.

Reno suddenly backed against the wall when he saw this stranger. "It's our father," he groaned, grasping Sitko by the shirttail to keep him away from the man.

But Sitko's fascination with this tall person who was his father was so great that he rushed forward and stood gazing up at him.

His father swept him up into his arms and held him close. Sitko was overwhelmed by the strange and marvelous smell of him. The man looked intently into Sitko's face, his lips twitching as if a flood of words was trying to free itself from his mind. But he said nothing. He put the little boy down and smiled sadly at Reno, as if he fully sensed his elder son's resentment.

Sitko slowly backed away, fearing his brother's disapproval. Reno clutched Sitko's hand and whispered something he could not understand.

"Have you been good fellows?" the man stammered, staring at Reno as if he hardly recognized the young man he had become.

Reno did not respond.

The pain in the man's face deepened. It hurt to look at him. Sitko thought the man would turn away, but he stood his ground and said falteringly, "Here . . . here . . . this is for you, Sitko. Go ahead . . . take it . . . it's for you."

Sitko glanced at Reno, but he did not move.

"Take it . . . take it," Reno finally muttered under his breath, releasing Sitko from his tight grasp.

The child slowly approached the tall man and took the package from his large hands.

The man bowed his head and then nodded apologetically to Reno. "I should have brought you something, too," he whispered.

"I don't want anything from you!" Reno exclaimed.

"Reno . . . you must try not to be so angry with me . . . you are too young to understand how these things happen," the father pleaded.

"I'm not mad at anybody," Reno said. "I don't care about your lousy gifts, and I'm not angry at anybody. So just leave us alone!"

Reno turned away. "Come," he called to Sitko. Then he started up the stairs.

Sitko began to follow Reno, but somehow he could not obey his brother. He could not give up this one chance of knowing this stranger who was his father.

"Sitko!" his brother shouted. "Come right now or you'll be damn sorry!"

Sitko was filled with an enormous longing to stay with his father, but he was afraid of losing his brother's love. Fathers go away and never come back. And if Sitko lost both his father and his brother, then he would have no one. Slowly he turned to follow Reno.

Then, all at once, the man took Sitko by the shoulders and would not let him go.

"Don't be afraid, Sitko," he said gently. "I must talk to you. You're such a little fellow you can't understand all of this, but you have to try to listen to me because I'm your father and I love you. Are you listening to me, Sitko?" he pleaded, with such intensity that Sitko was filled with pain and embarrassment for him.

"Sitko!" Reno shouted.

The child pulled against his father's grasp, trembling with confusion, but the man would not let him go. He held the child tightly as he began to speak quickly in an anxious voice.

"I don't want you to spend your childhood in a place like this. You need to have a family that loves you. Do you understand? It's different for Reno. He won't be here much longer, because in a couple more years he'll be out of school and have a job. But what will become of you then, Sitko? What will become of you?" his father repeated as he took both of Sitko's hands and pressed them to his chest. "So . . . you see . . . your mother . . . she wants you to have a home of your own. Your mother . . . she wants you to have a new daddy who can give you a nice home. He's a good man, Sitko. I've known him for a long time, and he promised me he would be a good father to you. He has a big house with lots of land, and I know that he will love you and give you the things I can't give you. Do you understand, Sitko, do you understand?"

Sitko shook his head violently at the thought that his own father was going to give him away to a stranger.

"No . . . no . . . no," Sitko cried, pulling away with all his might. "I hate you! I hate you!"

"My God, try to understand, Sitko! If Alexander Milas doesn't take you into his home, then somebody else will take you and you won't be able to see any of us ever again! Don't you see what I'm trying to say to you, Sitko?" his father exclaimed in a hoarse voice. "He wants to give you his name because he doesn't have a family of his own. He wants you to live with him in his big house because he doesn't have a wife and he doesn't have any children. He wants to be your father, Sitko. Dear God, I don't want to do this, but if I don't . . . then who knows who might adopt you. And we'll never see you again! You'll be stuck in this orphanage, and anybody . . . absolutely anybody will be able to take you! Anybody!"

Sitko watched with dread as his father's voice was swallowed up in his chest and he sank to his knees, covering his face with his hands and shaking with stifled sobs.

Suddenly Reno howled and ran up the stairs, his hands reaching desperately out into empty space. Sitko backed away in fear and confusion, staring at this tall man who was his father, crouched on his knees and sobbing.

The sky above Star of Good Hope filled with lightning and

whirlwinds. Sitko shuddered as he heard the thunder and felt the world tremble beneath his feet. Then the housemother came to his side. Without speaking, she quietly took Sitko by the hand. And as she led him away down the long, dark hallway, the child twisted around so he could take one last look at this man who was his father.

It was in the time of lightning and whirlwinds that Sitko Ghost Horse left Star of Good Hope and came to live in the house of Alexander Milas-Miller.

Looking back, he could see the child as he was led away from his brother. He could see Alexander Milas-Miller taking his hand and pulling him down the street, past the dormitory where Reno and he had lived . . . past the white house of the headmaster, beyond the little fountain where the boy and girl huddled beneath their green umbrella, and over the white line that the children were forbidden to cross. They went down the narrow road, past the grove of eucalyptus trees and the ruined Chinese garden, and out the gate by the railroad tracks. And when the train came, Alexander Milas-Miller led him into one of the wooden cars, and while Sitko looked out the dirty window, trying to understand the confusion and torment he felt, the train began to move farther and farther away from the Star of Good Hope, until at last it had vanished into the gray haze that rose like moonlight from the wide, honey-colored plains.

Looking back into the moonlight, Sitko could see a child alone. Looking back, he could see a boy with tears in his eyes. Looking back through the blaze of moonlight, he could see Alexander Milas-Miller leading him away. Even now, Sitko could still hear the desperate cry of that long-ago child. Far

35

beyond the world, somewhere in the deepest darkness, there was still the sound of the inconsolable howl of that abandoned child.

Great yellow machines rumbled in the splendid grass, opening wide brown bruises in the land and roaring angrily as mechanical arms tossed trees and stones into the summer air. The earth groaned and rolled over. Red ants and their squirming white grubs erupted through the surface and were blinded by the light. Horned lizards and spiders, dragonflies and field mice perished under grinding metal feet. And soon the familiar landscape vanished, leaving a terrible silence and countless rows of ugly little houses and flowers held prisoner by picket fences.

Plastic flamingos walked arrogantly across carefully manicured lawns, while electric toasters and Mixmasters hummed in chorus with washing machines and vacuum cleaners. Shopping carts rolled relentlessly through immense refrigerated markets. And Sitko watched in astonishment as crowds of jelly-filled people with powdered sugar smiles made an unbroken circle around him, turning the land of his childhood into a vast sea of small dreams and small aspirations.

When summer ended, Alexander Milas-Miller took Sitko Ghost Horse to the local elementary school.

"His name is Seymour Miller," he lied. "Sometimes they call him Sitko. He has some funny ideas, but he's a good boy, and I know you'll look after him for us."

Then, without another word, he left Sitko in the fearsome playground of childhood.

S I X

▲

Patu did not look at him. She silently placed his food upon the ledge. Then she hobbled slowly along the gray walls, muttering to herself. Words he could not understand. After circling the small room several times, she turned toward him, gazing at him with curiosity. As one person looks at another. Finally, she sighed with indifference or confusion or anger. He was not certain what her reaction meant.

"Eat," she said. "The prisoner should eat."

Then she turned away. And again, it was silent in the room.

"Thank you for bringing me food," he whispered, in the hope of winning her compassion.

Patu paid no attention to his remark. She leaned against the wall and slid to the floor, where she sat bundled in her robe, looking fixedly at the wall in front of her.

"I didn't mean to offend you," he said with caution.

The woman made no response.

"I didn't mean to upset you with my drawing."

Patu said nothing.

"The drawing on the wall . . ." Sitko continued slowly, pointing to the smudged image that hovered over them. "The drawing on the wall that offended you. I didn't know you would be angry if I made a picture of you."

Patu shrugged, but she did not look at him.

"In the city where I live . . . in the city the people like to have pictures made of them."

Patu huffed contemptuously under her breath and continued to stare at the wall.

"In the city they call the pictures *portraits*. The people in the city pay artists money to make portraits of them."

She made no response; so Sitko fell silent.

After a long time, Patu repeated: "Eat. The prisoner must eat."

Sitko nodded with resignation and crept across the floor to his bowl. As he put his fingers into the gruel and lifted it to his lips, he felt Patu's eyes turn toward him and fix upon his mouth. He ate in silence, keeping his attention on the bowl, realizing that with every morsel he ate the woman watched him more intently, waiting for the moment when he would offer the bowl to her.

"Here," he said. "Take it."

She grasped the bowl to her chest, holding it in both hands and gazing down at it, overwhelmed by hunger. But she would not eat while he watched her.

Sitko turned away and fixed his attention on the sunlit window. Only then could he hear the sounds of Patu eating.

Now, at last, he knew how he could reach her. So, with a new confidence, he said, "My name is Sitko."

But Patu made no response.

He turned to watch her as she fastidiously cleaned her motley whiskers and mouth. A cat after its meal. Then, without moving any closer to him, she extended her arms and thrust the bowl into his hands.

"Sitko," he repeated. "My name is Sitko."

She silently gazed at him for a long time, disregarding his statement. Then, quite suddenly, she stood up and walked to the door.

"Don't go," he urged. "I must talk to you."

Just as she was about to leave, she stopped and stood with her back to Sitko for a long time.

Sitko could hear nothing but the woman's breathing. Her body hunched forward as if she were consumed by an immense anger. Then the woman lurched, turning around and around, with her long black hair twisting about her face. As suddenly as she began, she stopped, standing massively just in front of Sitko and glaring at him.

"No portrait!" she exclaimed. "No more portrait!"

Sitko backed away from her, but she followed after him.

"It is my body! Not your body!" she exclaimed as she violently shook her head and mysteriously waved her hands in the air. Then, muttering and panting, she tore at the fastenings of her robe. With an outcry of anger and pain, she abruptly threw open her robe. For a moment she was silent. Then she whispered, "The spirit is in the body. *Spirit!* Do you understand? You make no pictures of the spirit!"

Sitko blinked in confusion as the words of the woman ran through his mind. Then he felt a terrible sense of mortification as he understood her meaning.

"I'm sorry . . ." he said, looking at her strong, chiseled face in the dim light of the little room. "I'm truly sorry," he repeated, realizing that tears were running down her cheeks. "I promise . . . no more pictures of your spirit."

Patu lowered her head, turning toward the sunlight coming in through the window.

It was only then that Sitko became aware of the woman's naked body, glistening like wet clay in the sunshine. She was very tall . . . perhaps six feet or more. She had broad shoulders and a barrel chest without muscular definition or breasts. Her belly was pithy and white. Her legs were massive and spaced far apart on her torso. One of them was badly scarred from mid-thigh to the ankle. And between her legs were not the genitals of a woman but a fragile penis that barely protruded from her flabby groin.

Sensing Sitko's astonishment, the woman quickly covered herself and leaned in exhaustion against the wall.

"I am a *katsotstsi,*" she murmured, sighing with great sorrow, as if she were profoundly weary of the world. "I am a *katsotstsi.* Do you understand?"

Sitko understood, but he did not know how to respond.

Slowly Patu lowered herself to the ground, where she sat so deeply bundled in her robe that Sitko could only see the top of her head.

"*Otstsi,*" she repeated softly. "I do not know how you say such things. We say *Lhamanaye* . . . powerful woman."

Sitko cautiously nodded. "Yes," he said.

"I take care of little children," she said. "When I was still young, I carried the little ones on my back in a blanket. I did not play with boys. I helped the mothers grind corn. I sang with the women. The boys ran free, chasing each other across all rooftops, climbing up and down the ladders of our houses, running down many covered passages, going wherever they wanted, in and out of all the rooms of houses."

"Yes," Sitko repeated, edging a bit closer to the woman.

"From the beginning I liked to play with dolls of baked clay or carved from cottonwood. In the spring, I went with many villagers on the rabbit hunt. And in the summer, the children rolled down the sand hills and jumped into the cold river. In the orchards, sometimes we stole peaches left to dry in the sun. If we got caught, the elders said we would be punished . . . and get eaten by monsters. But it was not true."

With this, Patu laughed, a large masculine laugh that was the first happy sound Sitko had heard in many days.

Now she looked at him with a timid smile. "But now I am not a child. I am *Lhamanaye* . . . powerful woman of the village."

"And do you have a family?"

"No . . . no family. I became *Lhamanaye*. A sacred person with no husband. When I was still a child, the Koyemshi came to our village, carrying Kaklo. *Kaklo, Kaklo, Kaklo.* That is what Kaklo always chants, as they carry him into our village. *Kaklo, Kaklo, Kaklo* . . . even when they go across the river and drop Kaklo and soil his beautiful white robes. *Kaklo, Kaklo, Kaklo.* Then in the sacred place with all us children, he told about the first beginning. And he chanted as he told how we began and how we will end our days. For a long time, he talked of the first beginning. And if a child nodded or fell asleep, Kaklo would hit that child on the head with the stuffed duck he always carried," Patu said with great delight.

"And you? Did you fall asleep?"

"No! I never fell asleep! This is a very serious time in the life of a child," Patu admonished gravely, the smile vanishing from her lips. "This is the Night of the Washing of the Hair.

A very serious time when mothers wash their children's hair and give new names to each of them. Then the spirits come to the village from the west, led by the great Horned Serpent. And then, in the main place, all the boys are whipped. So they will be forever brave men. But not me. I lived with the women who taught me many things. Grinding corn, making food like you eat in the bowl, cleaning house, fetching wood, carrying water, taking good care of the river gardens, making ceremonies. Then, when I became a grown person, I joined the masked dances. So now many people honor Patu because I am strong in body and spirit. I learned weaving. A woman gave me a lump of clay, and I wanted to change it into something. *'Good,'* the woman said to me. And she told me many sacred things. Clay is the flesh of earth. What is made from clay is flesh like me. Everything is alive. Things made from clay are alive, just like people."

For a moment Patu's face emerged from her robe and she gazed at Sitko. "Do you know clay?" she asked, in a cautious whisper.

Sitko responded with a gesture of confusion.

"No. You do not know clay. Because you are the evil one. Clay is a gift of the secret place. There is no evil there. The woman took me to the secret place when I became a powerful woman. The place of the Mother Rock. There my woman-teacher told me to tear off a little piece of my blanket and put it in a hole in the rock. But when we came near the home of the clay, the woman said to be quiet and not to move. She said, *'If we talk, the pottery will crack in the fire, and if we do not pray the clay will not come out of the earth.'* Then my teacher dug into the hard soil, all the time saying many prayers to Mother of the Earth. So we got much good clay this way.

We could make many fine pots. We fed the pots bread before putting them into the fire. We made prayers to the fire so it would not kill the pottery. And when the pot was finished, it became a living thing."

Sitko nodded as Patu waited for some sign of comprehension.

"Do you understand?" she asked gently.

"Yes . . ." he said. "Yes, I understand. It is the same for me when I make pictures."

"No. It is not the same," Patu insisted, with some impatience. "Your pictures are evil!"

"No, Patu. You must listen to me," Sitko urged. "Truly, it is the same. It is not what you think. My pictures are not evil. They are the same as when you make pottery."

"No. It is not true. It is not the same."

"Please, listen to me," Sitko insisted, sitting on the ground in front of Patu. "In the evenings I used to make pictures in a corner of the kitchen under my Grandma Amana's watchful eyes. And when I made pictures, I thought about emerald peacocks and misty pools . . . brilliant bursts of color in golden sunlight . . . water rippling and leaping . . . flowers and animals dissolving into a river of rainbows. And I tried again and again to make the marvelous pictures inside my head, but I could not get them to live on the paper. And when I became impatient and abandoned my drawings, Grandma Amana used to say, 'Do not be in such a hurry. Nothing can be born until it is ready.' "

Patu frowned intently and said: "This Grandma Amana was a wise woman."

"One day my Grandma Amana told me that it was time for my pictures to be born. So she gave me a brown paper bag

43

filled with crackers, and a bottle of water. And she gave me a bundle that was hidden away in the bottom of the string bag in which she kept all of her possessions. Then she told me it was time for me to go to the creek where powerful beings live, and to stay there all day and all night, and perhaps for another day and night."

Amana pressed Sitko forward, out the kitchen door, into the yard and down into the creek where the frogs and crickets joined in his grandmother's song . . . and where the Moon came down through the evening clouds and peered into his face to see if Sitko was the scar-faced child in whom the Morning Star shined.

It was night and it was cold. All the bark and wood he gathered was wet, and he could not start a fire. He sat in the darkness, surrounded by noises that came from deep within the crevices of the earth and among the high, black branches. He was frightened, but he sat perfectly still, trying to remember a song, trying to recall the words that Grandma Amana had taught him long, long ago. When he became very tired, he stood up and raised his arms, shaking them in the cold air so he would not fall asleep. And when footsteps resounded in the thickets he told his heart to be brave. When strange sounds surrounded him he reminded himself that all creatures were his brothers and that he belonged in their world with them, as they belonged in his. And when all the distant lights of the houses went out, and the headlights of automobiles vanished from the horizon, he shivered and prayed that he would not fail to open his heart to the gift that his grandmother had pleaded for him to receive from the night. By now, it was almost morning. The dew had come down upon the grass and the first birds of day were stirring and making their feeble peeping. Although he struggled to stay awake, he could not keep his eyes open. He felt mortified that he could not follow his grandmother's instructions, and he dug his fingernails into his palms in anger. The pain forced him to his feet. He opened his heart to the morning, and he tried to see the mist that was forming above the rushing, cold water of the creek. Then he sat down and filled his hands with grass, pulling it from the earth and rubbing it across his face. The smell filled his nostrils. He was overwhelmed by the sweetness of the grass, by the pungent warmth of the earth that clung to the delicate roots. And suddenly he heard it. A small voice somewhere just in front of him in the dimness of the dawn. He strained to see, but the light was so frail that he could not see. Gradually the sun came over the edge of the world and pointed its long golden fingers into a little clump of trees. He gasped and began to weep, for at last he could see what he prayed to see. His vision came from the burned-out trunk of an ancient tree. It was a small red fox with the eyes of a woman and the genitals of a man. He could see the animal only very vaguely at first, but as the wind came up and the clouds whirled into motion, the sky filled with an intense light, and in this storm of illumination he could see the animal very clearly. The fox crept from the old tree and posed motionlessly for a long time, peering at Sitko as if it knew him. He did not know why, but the sight of that powerful being made him cry out in pain. And at that very moment, the fox dashed into the dimness, flared up momentarily, turned first into a white bird and then into a particle of light cast into the emptiness of the sky.

"Hey!" Sitko shouted. "Don't leave me yet!"

But there was no reply. Sitko sat down dejectedly, fearing that he had lost his one encounter with the unknown.

Then suddenly something touched him.

He whirled around and found himself facing a pale, slender young man with bright red hair and deep green eyes.

"These are the things I give to you," he whispered without moving his lips. *"These are the things,"* he said, tracing something in the air with a long white finger, leaving glowing lines that hung in the air like fragrant smoke. *"These things are for you."*

When Sitko was completely surrounded by colors, the young man came very close to him and placed his frosty finger upon Sitko's forehead. The imprint remained forever upon his brow. And then he said, *"These colors will be your song."*

Then he was gone.

Patu nodded gravely, but she did not speak.

"I am no longer a boy," Sitko earnestly told her. "When I look into the mirror I am a tall, slender fellow with a child's hands and a grief-stricken face. Now when I am alone, my fingers release a downpour of rain and a blizzard of lightning and hail. Color and sparks are ignited by my fingers, and pictures gush from my hands. Slowly I have found my way back into the north country of my birth upon a white-and-purple highway that flows through my mind. Now my paintings fill me with an entirely new person I have never been before. Slowly I walk into the solitude of myself and I close the door behind me, shutting away everything that was painful and ugly. And for a time, before the sickness came, I was safe."

Patu and Sitko sat on the ground and gazed at one another, like distant stars in the dark immensity of the sky, desperately flashing their frail messages across the unthinkable distance that separated them.

Finally, Patu drew her arms about her shoulders, as if she suddenly felt intensely cold.

"Every night I hear much crying," she said. "Every night this crying comes from the place where the children are kept until we understand what kind of creature you are. But the crying also comes from this room. A terrible, sad sound from this room where you stay. Like the sound of a child. And this crying makes me very sad, for I am a powerful woman who loves all the children. And all the children love Patu. But from this room, every night, I hear the crying of a lost child. A frightened child. And I want to make the child not to cry. So I say to my people, 'Maybe this man is not evil. For evil does not know how to cry. So maybe this man is not the evil one who brings many bad things to our village.' But the Two Horn Priests, they say, 'Maybe he is very clever, and weeps just to fool us!' So I do not know," Patu murmured with confusion, studying Sitko's eyes.

Sitko sighed, and then he said: "There are people who want to believe in evil."

"You are very clever," Patu whispered and smiled warily. "I must be careful of you," she said, as she struggled to her feet, collected Sitko's bowl, and hobbled toward the door. "I think, perhaps, you are too clever to be good."

Then the door closed behind her.

SEVEN

▲

PATU GAZED AT Sitko Ghost Horse. She placed his bowl of food upon the ledge, and then she looked at him with a perplexed expression in her black eyes. Sitko gave her little notice. He was completely concentrated upon the lines that flowed from his fingertips.

Patu quietly moved along the walls, whispering to herself. Perhaps it was a song or a prayer. Sitko heard her voice, but he did not take his attention from his fingers.

After slowly circling the small room, Patu crept up behind Sitko and cautiously peered over his shoulder. His fingers were luminous as they moved. Something amazing was happening. Sitko was using the charcoal and chalky stone Patu had given him to make something on a scrap of cardboard. Patu sighed in astonishment, for, as she watched, the legs and the body of a deer were being born upon the paper. Soon even the nose and the slender ears of the creature appeared, until, finally, its mystery-filled eyes looked up at her.

"How does a stranger from the other world, how does he do such a thing as this?" she questioned softly, speaking more to herself than to her prisoner. Then she laboriously circled Sitko where he sat hunched upon the ground. She whispered to herself. And, finally, she gently nudged him with her withered foot.

"This thing you do . . ." she murmured with confusion, "this is like the long-ago days when we understood the animals. Very long ago. It is like the legend days, when holy people got power from spirit-animals. I remember winters long ago when people danced and danced . . . until they got strong . . . and then they could hear the words of some great animal that gave power to their lives."

Without taking his attention from his work, Sitko mumbled: "Tell me about the legend days."

"Oh, it is a long time since the legend days. Long time. Nothing left of the legend days. No good air. The land is dead now. Animals are always silent to us. No dancing. No songs. No dreaming. Now nothing is left of the legend days but these marks . . . here on my fingers," Patu explained, holding out her strong hands and indicating the lines etched into the flesh of her fingertips. "It is the wind that gave all the creatures life. It is the breath of life. It is the wind that comes out of our mouths now that makes us live. When this wind stops blowing, then we die. We die and we are gone. But here . . ." Patu murmured, gazing at her fingers, "here in the skin of our fingertips we see the trail of the wind." And then she made a circular motion to indicate the whirlwind that had left its imprint in the whorls at the tips of the human finger. "It shows where the wind blew life into my ancestors when they were first made. . . . It was in the legend days when these lines happened. It was in the legend days when the first people were given the breath of life."

Sitko leaned against his knees and looked up at Patu, listening intently to her story and watching in delight as her large hands moved delicately through the air, transforming her odd, massive body into a great splash of shadow upon the gray wall. It was a magical light. And it was a familiar light. Like summer evenings in the orchard surrounding the house of Alexander Milas-Miller. A light filled with the drone of insects and the chatter of birds.

Looking back in the summer's light, Sitko could see Patu merging with the sunset, first turning into flame and then changing into darkness. Now, in the gloom, the great Sun himself stepped into the gray room, blazing upon the walls. The same dazzling Sun also climbed into the sky above the house of Alexander Milas-Miller. Sitko could hear the mockingbirds that sang to one another across the vast fields of golden grass and pink hollyhocks. He could see Grandma Amana sitting in the luminous evening, telling stories as she cut vegetables for dinner, slowly turning string beans and potatoes in her wrinkled brown hands.

Looking back, Sitko could see Grandma Amana in the evening, kneeling by his bed and praying that his father, Jamie Ghost Horse, would come back and take his family to a house of their own.

Looking back, Sitko could also hear the breathing of his mother somewhere in the night. He could hear her troubled breathing when she came into his bedroom and stood silently in the darkness of the house of Alexander Milas-Miller. Sitko could hear his mother as she paced back and forth and wept.

He pretended to be asleep. But he could not sleep while his mother wept and the house of Alexander Milas-Miller was filled with his grandmother's urgent prayers. He could not sleep in the dark, when the Sun vanished from the world, and the night held him captive in the lodge of the Moon.

The lodge of the Moon was a place made of gleaming white stone. It was a fierce and terrible place. Hanging everywhere within her lodge were countless eyes—the eyes of those she had taken prisoner. She had taken out their shining eyes and hung them in her lodge.

Now these disembodied eyes dangled helplessly as they frantically watched Sitko. He cautiously backed away from the dreadful lodge of the Moon, trying to find his way through the darkness to the bed where he slept. But suddenly the Moon leaped from a great black tree. Sitko howled in fear as the Moon's long white wings exploded into crystals of frozen light.

She shrieked and peered down into Sitko's dream. And she blinked her great white eyes and laughed. *"Your agony will not end here, you bastard-boy!"* she shouted. *"It follows after you and sinks its teeth into your heart. You are dying! Bastard-child! Can't you feel the death in your body, hatching its ten million eggs inside your eyes?"*

Sitko screamed with fear.

"You squealing little bastard! Did you think you could fool the Moon? You pathetic half-thing! Did you think that I would ever let you be free?" she shouted, twisting her glittering mouth into a leer and howling as she jabbed out at him with her jagged claws and ripped across his face.

"Ah!" he screamed in pain, the blood pouring over his cheek and blinding him. "Ah!" he wailed, backing away deliriously and trying to wipe the blood from his eyes. "Oh, no!" Sitko cried out, as he fell back and stumbled with a groan, grappling blindly, clutching the fierce wound on his face, and staggering in retreat as the Moon tossed her blazing crystals at him. "Ah!" he cried desperately, as he hurtled into the darkness, yelling frantically and running away from that terrible sight of the Moon. Falling. Falling . . . falling . . . falling again and again. Colliding in the dark with monstrous, shapeless things . . . collapsing at the edge of a bubbling yellow river . . . and calling out and sobbing until the night turned orange and scarlet and purple . . . and black.

Sitko groaned in terror when he awoke. He could see two little eyes very close to him. He abruptly sat up and shouted. Suddenly a great flock of yellow birds leaped into the air with a rush of wings. A fierce wind blew over him.

Then it was morning. And Patu looked down at him with a smile.

"You need food," she said, handing him his bowl.

Sitko placed the food on the ground, between them, and he said: "Let us eat together."

Patu shyly turned away, mumbling self-consciously and covering her mouth with a delicate gesture.

"Please . . ." he entreated. "Share my food with me."

For a while she did not respond. But then she crept across the floor and took a position across from him, looking at him falteringly with great uncertainty and caution.

"Sometimes . . ." Patu said slowly, "sometimes I think I know you. And sometimes I see you clearly. Sometimes I think maybe you really are who you say you are."

Sitko smiled with gratitude. Then he said, "I am one of the leftover people. It is true," he murmured, "I belong nowhere and I belong to no one. I have no family. And all my friends are gone. But I have one thing that no one can take from me. My grandmother put something into my heart. Within me, very deep inside of me, I possess a world that other people cannot see, a place where the light is blue. And nothing can ever put out the blue flame that Grandma Amana lighted within me."

The flame came into the gloomy little prison, rising between Sitko and Patu and lighting the room. A house made of dawn. The light had no bounds. So great was the blue flame Grandma Amana had ignited in Sitko that it could illuminate all that ever was and all that ever would be. Somewhere in the sky that boundless light still recalled all the countless moments of the world, large and small. In its deathless memory the light remembered every bird and mountain and star, and carried those memories endlessly through all the senseless circles of time.

Looking back into the light, Sitko could still see Grandma Amana smiling at him.

"*Au-wah-tsahps* . . . screwball," she had murmured in his ear. When he embraced her he was overcome by the fragility of her tiny body, by the helplessness of her twisted fingers and the frail light that still glowed in her ancient eyes. Those eyes, full of strength and fear and death, still haunted Sitko. When he looked into them he plummeted into the light—falling endlessly through every day that had ever existed. In his grandmother's eyes there were three hundred sunrises and ten thousand starlit nights. In her eyes were the beginning of the world and the last golden light of the final Sun.

"You are a good boy," she whispered.

As he embraced her again, he could feel her bones pressing

through her emaciated flesh. And in the long folds of her throat he could see her pulse tugging desperately at life, fighting to keep her body alive.

". . . a good boy."

But Sitko was no longer a boy. When he looked into the mirror he saw a tall, slender young man with a child's hands and a grief-stricken face. He hated what he saw in the mirror. His coarse black hair. His dark skin. His large nose and square jaw. He loved things that were beautiful. But the young man in the glass was not beautiful. And so he tried to look beyond the surface of the looking glass, through and beyond its fragile reflections, and into the light itself . . . the blue light that streamed boundlessly through all the circles of time.

Only when he was able to find his way into that world of endless light was he truly happy. Then he could recreate in his drawings and watercolors all the things he saw in the bright light beyond the looking glass. And so, until the day he went away to art school, he stayed in the blue flame of Grandma Amana, where the light was always strongest. He stayed in the kitchen and listened to her stories of the long-ago legend days . . . when people were as beautiful as eagles. He gazed at her luminous face as she told him about the good days when her people were beautiful and free.

"We had many horses and we were strong . . . oh, so very strong!" Grandma Amana murmured. "We had so many good days. But now, look at us. We have nothing."

Sitko watched as his grandmother's eyes filled with memories. Her face was as wrinkled and brown as a turtle's. She seemed like the oldest person in the world, but her wonderful dark eyes shined with youth.

She laughed as she dropped a potato into the big pot of

water and it made a splash. And then Grandma Amana drew in her breath, and the blue light appeared within her body as she sat in the kitchen peeling potatoes and dropping them into the pot. She closed her eyes to summon a story from within her body, and then she began to speak.

"One day, when the strangers were still few and the grass did not know their angry feet and the land did not know their grasping hands, there were many animals and many good things of the earth for all to eat. The animals talked to us. They were our teachers, giving us the old wisdom that turned the earth green and brang rain and sunshine. These were good days. But the grass began to die and the animals no longer spoke to us. The land was filled with strangers, and there were no more good days for us. Ah, the wind stirs the willows! Listen to it, my son. Fog! Lightning! Whirlwind! The rocks are ringing, they are ringing from the tall mountains. Now the Sun's yellow beams are running out. Great Sun is dying. But we shall live again. We shall live again!"

Sitko looked into the old woman's eyes, astounded by the courage and passion he found in them. As he sank into her gaze, he entered her world of bright yellow thoughts, like the place in the acorn that imagines the tree.

Looking into her eyes, he always saw that marvelous place where music and pictures and books were born. The thought of that place overwhelmed him. He gasped and shook his head in bewilderment. And as he shook his head, the brightness of his mind turned gray. Then it changed again. Into a wall.

He stared at the wall where the traces of a large woman still lingered. In this gray little room. In his prison. In that terrible place at the center where the light and all that it remembered seemed to die in the mouth of darkness.

Again he shook his head. He did not realize that he was weeping until he felt tears running down his cheeks. Yet again he shook his head, like a swimmer emerging from a deep stream. And he sighed when he recognized Patu sitting quietly before him.

They did not speak. He watched her, fascinated as she changed and changed.

Finally, as the light began to fail, he pressed his bowl of food into Patu's hands. She accepted it reluctantly, lowering her head in a gesture of gratitude. Then she looked up at him with a great tenderness.

He nodded at her and said: "It was in the time of lightning and whirlwinds that my brother, Reno, came to live with me and my mother and my Grandma Amana in the house of Alexander Milas-Miller."

In the evening, Sitko unrolled his secret pictures and showed them to Reno. His brother looked intently at the images that Sitko had created from the tales he had read to him. Reno said nothing, but Sitko knew he was pleased, for a wisp of a smile crossed his serious face and his eyes brightened.

"What is this?" Reno asked as he lifted another picture into the light and studied it. "What story is this?"

Sitko was reluctant to answer because the drawing was not about one of Reno's stories.

"It's okay, you can tell me. What is this supposed to be?"

Sitko looked away. He was afraid to answer his brother's question. The picture was about something lost, something that the light remembered but that everyone else had lost.

"Tell me, what is it, Sitko? Is it a story of your own?"

It was the picture of a tall, dark man standing in a doorway. It was a picture of their father as he still lived in Sitko's drawings.

When Sitko finally told his brother the truth, Reno did not get angry. He sat back sadly and fell silent as he continued to look at the picture. Then, at last, he said in a gentle voice, "I remember when I was maybe seven years old. Before you were born. Our father and I helped build a little monument on the side of the highway. It was a monument for soldiers who had died in some past war. I don't know which war it was, but it was the one that happened a long time ago, when our father was still young. He used to get together with a bunch of men and on Sundays they would dig a lot of holes and pour cement and work on this little monument by the side of the road. I don't know where it is. But I bet you anything it's still standing somewhere out by the highway, half covered with weeds."

Reno reached hesitantly toward the picture, touching it with the tips of his fingers and then drawing them to his lips. "I like to remember that monument, because nobody else knows anything about it. Just me. There's not a living person in the world who remembers that monument and how we used to work on it. But everything else from those days is gone," Reno said dolefully. Then he shrugged and laughed dryly. "Y'know, Jamie Ghost Horse was always puffed up about being Indian. Our mom, she hated being Indian. Never would admit to it. Not to this day. But our dad, he thought he was Geronimo or something. But he didn't know the first thing about it. Took me a long time to realize it, but I finally saw he was just full of hot air. Grandma Amana, now she really spoke the language and she grew up with it, but Jamie—well, he was just proud of being Indian 'cause he didn't have anything else to be proud about. He's what they call a *renegade*. All he knew for sure was that he could drink a pint of booze faster than you could pour it. And when he wasn't drunk he was running off with the rodeo. No credit and lots of bills. Everywhere we went, they came looking to get some money from us. Jamie called himself by all kinds of names in those days. I don't even remember half the names we used to use. That's why none of us know who the hell we really are. He dragged me and Mom around with him in his truck. He worked in circuses and rodeos and anything else that would keep him in booze. Sometimes he came home with us. But most of the time he stayed away. I don't know how Mom put up with it for as long as she did. She was maybe sixteen when they got married. She thought he was some kind of big hero. Good-looking and all that. But she found out that he was just a renegade and a damn drunk. Then you were born and we stayed put for a while. But that didn't last long. Finally he just walked out on us," Reno said bitterly, as he slowly wadded up the picture in his fist and held it to his chest with both hands.

"So now you know all about our father," he muttered shamefully, without looking at Sitko. "Now you know."

E I G H T

▲

SITKO GHOST HORSE awakened with a start. Instantly he leaped to his feet, crouching close to the ground, ready to defend himself or to take flight.

It was still dark. And it was silent.

He shook his head in confusion. What had jolted him from sleep? Had there been a crash? A scream? A call for help?

Perhaps not. Perhaps it was a dream. For it seemed to him that some dreadful, unbearable fear had followed him into the world from sleep. But he could recall nothing of his dreams. Only a stupefying fear that violently hissed through his limbs like an electrical shock.

He sank to the ground. Exhausted. Still trembling from the terror that had seized him. So exhausted, but too frightened to close his eyes and return to sleep, where the thing that had terrified him still lingered.

He assured himself that everything was all right. Very soon it would be dawn. Sunlight would return to the little room,

59

and he could make a picture. That always made him feel better.

He sat up slowly and peered cautiously into the shadows of the room, possessed by a lingering fear . . . an utterly pointless but overwhelming fear.

Still it was silent. Still it was dark.

Then, to his astonishment, he noticed that the door of his prison was slightly ajar. Impossible. Perhaps the darkness was playing tricks on his eyes. "No," he murmured, "the door is open. . . ."

His first thought was to escape. He was seized by an incredible excitement as that thought overtook him. He moistened his dry lips and breathed hard as he crept toward the door, trembling with the anticipation of racing across the dark plain to freedom. But as he approached the door, he hesitated.

What if they were testing him? What if they were waiting out there in the night, watching to see what he would do? What if they were out there, ready to catch him, ready to say that only the guilty run away?

His hopes collapsed. His body, which had been galvanized by the possibility of freedom, became limp and helpless. Now he felt trapped. Resigned to captivity. Unable to make a decision or to take any action. He hated what was happening to him. But he no longer knew what to do.

He crouched on the floor and waited to be summoned. But no one came for him. He slept fitfully a moment at a time, awakening with the same electrical jolt of fear that had tormented him earlier. He groaned and opened his eyes. It was still the middle of the night. It had been at just such a time of day that he had been summoned to his first interrogation.

Perhaps they were waiting for him. Perhaps he was expected to prove himself one way or the other. Flee and admit guilt or stay and defend himself. Surely that was it! Just as he had suspected, they were testing him! The open door. The moonless night. The hour for another interrogation. Or time for an escape. Clearly, it was a test, and they were out there, waiting to see what he would choose to do.

Sitko Ghost Horse laughed out loud. He would not submit himself to their ridiculous games. Not for a moment more. He stood up resolutely and brushed the dust from his filthy clothes. He would show them how an innocent person behaves! A marvelous vitality ran through his body once again. His mind was cleansed by a cascade of light, and he felt in full possession of his life. It was a marvelous feeling—a sensation that he had not experienced since the days before the sickness came. He laughed again and started toward the open door. Now he knew exactly what he must do.

He strode into the darkness without the least timidity, looking neither to the right nor to the left. He went by himself, willingly and unbound, to the same underground chamber where his first interrogation had taken place. In the dark corridors, people crouched senselessly, staring into space. In the courtyards, gray figures stood motionless and silent. No one gave the least notice to Sitko. It was as if he no longer existed. Their empty eyes were chilling.

Without a moment's delay, he hurried on his way to the interrogation room.

Then he stopped short. Turning a corner, he abruptly came upon a corpse lying on the ground in a cotton frock extending from the neck to the feet. Sitko drew back in wonderment and fear, staring at the body. It was the body of a young man not more than twenty years old, with a faint mustache just beginning to bud on his lip—tall, muscular, and handsome. A bandage was tied under his chin to hold his jaw closed; his thin wrists were secured across his chest, and his fingers held a small clay pot. On each side of his head was a lighted candle, and ants were swarming across his pallid face, disappearing into his nostrils.

All at once a mournful sound filled the courtyard and a small procession made its way past Sitko. The corpse of the young man was gently lifted by the robed figures as they chanted. Sitko stumbled along beside the procession until it reached a rude little grave. There they paused in silence.

When two men lifted the youth's body, the head turned to one side and the hands dropped and swung freely. The miserable grave was too short, and as the corpse was laid into it the legs buckled and the knees came up in a grotesque posture. Sitko gazed at the young man's face. There were long welts and bruises on his cheek, and there was a delicate noose around his neck. Death had left nothing but a pathetic smile on the boy's lips. It was a dreadful sight, but Sitko could not turn away.

The old men who had put the corpse into the grave mumbled to one another as they retreated. Only one woman remained. She began to scrape up soil in her hands and throw it on the corpse. The body was very gradually covered, so slowly and meticulously that Sitko became mesmerized by what he was witnessing. At first the feet stuck out, and then all was buried but the face. A small piece of muddy soil fell upon one of the eyes, and another on the boy's smiling mouth, changing the whole expression in a moment, so that he was suddenly possessed by his death.

The old woman stopped for a moment and seemed to lament the terrible change that had come over the corpse. Then the dirt fell on the face, covering everything but the nose. And then the young man was gone—as if he had never existed, as if his life had meant nothing.

Now the sky was filled with outcries and lamentations. Several hogs swarmed into the courtyard, which was afloat with sewage. A woman came out of her hut. She ignored Sitko as she called in a harsh voice for her children. Child after child straggled home, and each was piled atop the others on the filthy floor of the hut.

The Moon rose slowly. Birds costumed the night and their cries filled the darkness. The woman remained in the doorway of her hut, staring relentlessly at Sitko, who stood stupefied in her intense gaze. Without taking her eyes from him, she lighted a cigar and puffed on it deliberately. Then she drove off the hogs and retreated into her hut.

Sitko closed his eyes for a moment, trying to gather his energy and to forget the terrible image of the dead young man. Slowly he turned from the courtyard, and then he began to run. He searched through the black passages and stairways, looking for the hatchway and the ladder that led into the subterranean interrogation room. He soon came to the right place.

The door opened at once to his knocking, and without seeing the dwarf who remained standing by the door, he made straight down the ladder.

"No meeting . . . no meeting now," the dwarf said.

"Why is there no meeting?" Sitko demanded with some irritation.

The dwarf made a gesture of confusion. Then he pointed

into the dim chamber below as if to prove his point. It was empty. The platform where Sitko had been forced to stand and give his testimony was gone. In its place was a structure that might have been an altar. On the altar were several books.

Without the slightest hesitation, Sitko approached the altar and asked: "May I look at these books?"

"No," the dwarf replied. "That is not allowed."

"I see," Sitko said, in a tone of exasperation. "That's nonsense, isn't it. Undoubtedly those books are about your laws. They probably contain information that would help me. But, apparently, in this village a person is judged despite both his innocence and his ignorance."

"Yes . . ." the dwarf stammered, apparently not understanding Sitko's sarcasm.

"Well, in that case I might as well go back to my prison," Sitko said with irritation, realizing all at once that he had acted foolishly in coming to the meeting room instead of trying to escape. "I'm not going to accomplish anything here."

"No!" the dwarf entreated with a burst of emotion that surprised Sitko. "Stay with me. I can help you."

Sitko cautiously observed the little man, whose narrow eyes and tiny knob of a nose struck him as rather pathetic. The ceremonial mud that had covered the dwarf's head at the interrogation had been washed away. And whereas he had seemed utterly demonic during Sitko's interrogation, now he seemed pitiable, even ridiculous.

"Do you really want to help me?" Sitko asked.

"Oh, yes! I want to help! It is bad here," the dwarf said after a cautious pause, taking Sitko's hand. "You are from outside; so you know. You are the only one who knows how horrible it is here. So I want to help."

Sitko smiled and twisted his hand around within the dwarf's soft palm. "Perhaps you really can help me," he said.

"What can I do? How can I help?" the dwarf urgently asked.

"First of all, by letting me look at the books on the altar."

"Of course!" the dwarf exclaimed, pulling Sitko hastily to the altar.

The books were in a terrible state, discolored, dog-eared, and covered with filth.

"How dirty everything is here!" Sitko said in disgust.

The dwarf gazed at Sitko apologetically and hurriedly wiped away the dust before gesturing for Sitko to approach the altar.

Sitko expectantly opened the first book. On the first page he found a pornographic picture. A man and a woman sitting naked on a sofa, clutching at each other's genitals. The drawing technique and perspective were so terrible that Sitko found the picture more laughable than indecent. He had expected to find answers to his quandary. In dismay and disappointment he closed the book without looking at any other pages. But before turning away from the altar, he glanced at the second book. It was a romance novel entitled *Dark Secrets and Lurid Dreams*. Sitko sneered. Clearly his situation was hopeless. How could he defend himself against such people?

Turning to the dwarf but talking to himself, Sitko muttered: "*These* are the books that are studied here? *These* are the men who are going to sit in judgment of me?"

"I will help! I will help!" the dwarf insisted with great urgency.

"And what in the world can you do? What can anyone do in such a ridiculous situation? And even if you could be of some help to me, can you do it without getting yourself into terrible trouble?"

"I want to help, all the same," the dwarf insisted, glancing uneasily around the chamber, as if he were saying something which was risky both to him and to Sitko. "Come, let us talk. Do not worry for me. Come."

The dwarf settled himself on the floor and made room for Sitko beside him. When they were seated, the little man gazed up at Sitko. "You have beautiful dark eyes," he said. "I have been told that my eyes are beautiful, but yours are nicer. I liked you as soon as I saw you, the first time you came here. And that is why I want to help."

"So that's what this is all about," Sitko thought, standing up impatiently. "I really don't think you can help me," he said.

"No!" the dwarf cried, tightly grasping Sitko's hand. "Please do not go away! Could you do that to me? Am I so ugly and stupid that you won't do me the kindness of staying a little longer?"

"You misunderstand," Sitko said, sitting back down. "If you want me to stay I'll stay. I have nowhere to go. They left my door open. I don't know why. I came here expecting to find a meeting. I came here to prove my innocence. But I was mistaken. Now I don't care about any of this foolishness. There's nothing you can do to help me, unless you want to guide me out of this horrible place. I don't care what your people think of me. They have no right to sit in

66

judgment of me, and I would only laugh at them if they were to find me guilty of some crime I have not committed. I was foolish to come here. I don't know what I was thinking. Sometimes I fear that I'm losing my mind. This whole situation is nonsense . . . complete nonsense. *For those who are walled up everything is a wall, even an open door.* What I should have done tonight is what any sane person would have done. I should have run for my life!"

"I could help you do that," the dwarf exclaimed. "I would show you the way . . ." Suddenly he broke off, laying his hand on Sitko's knee as if to reassure him, and whispered: "Hush, someone is watching us."

Sitko slowly raised his eyes. In the hatchway, in the shadows at the top of the ladder, was a massive figure. The person stepped forward into the light. It was Patu.

The dwarf quickly bent over Sitko and whispered, "Do not be angry with me, but I must go now." He gave Sitko's hand a last caress, jumped up onto his stumpy legs, and clumped off into the darkness that clouded the space behind the altar.

Patu showed no surprise at finding Sitko in the subterranean chamber, and she took no notice of the fleeing dwarf. She simply said, "It is time for your food. Come."

Sitko followed after Patu without speaking, moving through dim passageways and up and down a maze of staircases until they came out in the open field where the solitary prison room was located.

It was dawn. Narrow threads of light made their way across the dark landscape, like a network of gleaming nerves and tendrils. A living thing. Unwillingly accepting their weight. As they crossed the field, the earth beneath Sitko's feet felt like flesh. The sensation was at once pleasurable and grotesque. He was consumed by the experience, utterly numbed by it. And now it seemed to him that the closer he came to his prison, the more he lost his determination to be free.

Sitko and Patu staggered forward. The distance between them and the prison seemed to grow with each step they took. Then the dusky landscape began to turn crimson as the Sun edged over the craggy horizon, sending a great fire into the world. The desolate wasteland groaned as the blaze lacerated the endless fields of broken rocks, dead trees, and whirling dust devils. The ground seemed to die and turn to crystal, becoming unbearably hot beneath their feet as they made their way toward the solitary little building where Sitko was held prisoner. Three large buzzards circled slowly in the burning sky. And a sickening stench of death and decay filled the air. Sitko held his hand over his nose and mouth as he followed after Patu, stepping between the carcasses of dead donkeys lying on their bloated sides, their stiff legs jutting out. A million flies flitted over their swollen, protruding tongues and swarmed over their large, brown, open eyes.

Finally Sitko and Patu reached the prison. On each side of the doorway stood a Two Horn Priest. The door was still ajar, although no one took any notice. Patu made a commanding gesture, waving the priests to one side. They resentfully backed off, muttering and complaining but too fearful of Patu to contest her authority. Once Sitko and Patu entered the prison, the door instantly banged shut and the lock made a loud noise as it was bolted.

Patu silently brought the food bowl from the ledge, placed it on the ground, sat down, and waited for Sitko to join her. Without looking at one another, they passed the bowl back and forth, dipping their fingers in the gruel and eating without pleasure in the forlorn atmosphere of the little room. For a very long time neither of them spoke. Finally, Patu said matter-of-factly: "You made a very bad impression on the elder. . . ."

"He's an ugly old man and I don't give a damn what kind of an impression I made on him or on anybody else for that matter!" Sitko muttered, still avoiding Patu's eyes, feeling embarrassed . . . somehow feeling embarrassed that she might realize he had contemplated escaping when he awakened and found the door of his prison open.

"This ugly old man . . . he has much power over the village. Not good power. He has power because all the people fear him. He is called Delito. And he is scheming and he is brutal and he is much feared. He likes to be feared. In all his life he has tried to be many things, but he failed in everything. The only thing he can do well is to scheme and to make people fear him. I have known Delito for a long time. As you say . . . he is old and ugly. And you are young and beautiful. For you, that is good, but for Delito that is not good. He cannot bear the spirit living inside of you, looking out at him through your wonderful eyes. It horrifies him. *To be nothing more than innocent!* How it angers Delito! *Pale ire, envy, and despair.* It doesn't matter if you are good or if you are evil. That does not matter to him. It is enough that he can hate you. And for you, my friend, that is a misfortune. Because it is Delito who must decide that you are good and not evil before the people will let you go."

"But that's nonsense! I haven't done anything wrong. And I don't have to prove my innocence to anybody!"

"Then they will not let you go. . . ."

"They can't keep me here forever," Sitko exclaimed.

"No," Patu murmured, "they will not keep you forever. That is not what they will do."

"And what is it that they think they can do to me?" Sitko asked with unbridled sarcasm.

"They will kill you."

Sitko stared at Patu, unable to believe what she had said. But once he saw her solemn expression, his defiance turned to apprehension and panic. "You do not mean it . . . surely you don't really mean it," he whispered.

After a long pause, Patu sadly repeated the words: "Yes, they will kill you. If they decide you are evil, the priests will kill you."

"But that's impossible! How can they kill an innocent person? How can they do such a thing? What right do they have to do such a terrible thing!"

Patu nodded helplessly and with a gesture of finality said, "It is our way."

"Your way? *Your way!* What kind of people are you? Good lord, just what kind of people live in this village?"

"They are good people," Patu said. "They do not want to hurt anyone. But you crossed the lines of pollen that close the roads to our village; you came here at a forbidden time, on the Night of the Washing of the Hair. For us, that is bad. For this village, that is something very bad."

"Why is it bad? How was I to know that strangers are not supposed to come here?" Sitko demanded.

"We do not talk of it," Patu murmured. "It is forbidden."

"Good lord, for you everything is forbidden!"

"We only say *Astotokya* . . . the Night of the Washing of the Hair. It is very sacred. And we do not speak of it."

70

"But how can I defend myself if I don't know what I'm supposed to have done?" Sitko insisted. "For godsake, how can I defend myself?"

Patu made a gesture of caution and hushed him. Then she crept to the door and listened carefully for the voices of the Two Horn Priests.

"They have much power," Patu whispered, as she edged back to Sitko's side. "They fear me only because I am *kat-sotstsi* . . . because I am *Lhamanaye* . . . a powerful woman in the body of a man. But they would take my power if they could. They want me to be nothing. So I am careful."

Sitko nodded and put his hand over his lips, nervously saying, "Okay . . . okay . . . I won't make any noise. I promise I won't make any noise. But tell me what is happening here . . . tell me what is going on in this village."

As he spoke his voice filled with urgency, and Patu hushed him once again.

"Okay . . . okay," he murmured. "Okay . . ."

"I will tell," Patu whispered. "I will tell you of the Night of the Washing of the Hair."

Sitko anxiously awaited as Patu drew closer and began to speak so softly that he had to hold his breath in order to hear her words.

"Every four years," she whispered, "when the sky is filled with the drumming of the Moon, then we have *Astotokya*. When there is the full Moon, then the young people are ready to be born. Then they become real people."

"Like an initiation?" Sitko asked with confusion. "Is that what it is? Like an initiation when the young people become adults?"

"Yes . . . like that," Patu whispered. "For us they are the

first people of the world, like our ancestors who came to this village when everything happened for the first time. The young ones are like our ancestors . . . clean and new. No evil. No sickness. Perfect first people of the world. But perfect first people must be kept clean. So we make Closing of the Roads with dust made of pollen."

"You make lines in the roads? Is that it? You seal off your village from strangers?" Sitko asked. "Is that what has happened?"

"Yes . . . like you say, close off strangers."

"And what happens to your young people?"

"The young ones are put alone in a deep chamber in the east side of the village. Everybody leaves there. Nobody stays in the east of the village. All the people are kept away except the priests and the good spirits who come to our village to bless the children. The deep chamber is called One-Way Path, because it is the place below the land where creation happened and the first people came out. There is just one hole in the chamber, the roof door on top of the ladder. Not until the secret ceremony is finished and children are blessed by the ancestors can they come out. Until the blessing, they must stay in the chamber long days and nights."

"And then what happens?" Sitko urged.

"Good things happen when they are blessed. But terrible things happen sometimes. If any person breaks through the closed roads of the village, all children in the chamber are made sick with evil. No child or priest will come out of the chamber alive."

"For godsake, what are you saying? Do you mean to tell me that just because I accidentally stumbled into this village . . . just because I happened to come to this godforsaken place all those people are going to be killed? Is that what you're telling me?"

Patu looked away and nodded sadly. "When the children and the priests go into the chamber, the One Horn Priests and the Two Horn Priests guard the empty village streets. Nobody is allowed outside. If the priests hear something or see something, they call out: *'Haqumi?'* Who are you? At once there is an answer, *'Pinu'u,'* I am I, which is the way the good spirits speak when they come to our village. But if there is no answer or a human person is found, then the One Horn Priests run and stab the evil one with their long lances, and they tear apart the body and run all night in every direction and bury some of the flesh in secret places."

Sitko was trying to comprehend the things Patu was telling him. After a moment, he asked, "Is that what happened to me?"

Patu nodded gravely.

"But the Two Horn Priests didn't try to kill me."

"You do not understand," Patu said in a whisper, gesturing cautiously toward the door. "The One Horn Priests did not find you. It was the Two Horn Priests. They are not like the One Horn Priests. They are much more sacred. They ran to you, trying to reach you before the One Horns, to capture you and protect you until Delito could decide if you are good or if you are evil. If evil, then you and the children and even the priests will die. But if you are good, then the young ones will come out of the deep chamber with the priests, and water will be poured on top of them, washing away all sickness and evil. Naked and wet like babies born into the first world, the children will come to powerful women like me. Then we will wash their hair with nine bowls of suds made from the yucca. And then the roads will be opened and life begins again."

Sitko Ghost Horse could hear someone weeping. The muffled sounds of weeping were everywhere. A frantic feeling overran his mind. Like a dream. Like a dream of the dead. A world of dead children. A world of stinking, decomposing children. Beyond the window of his prison, somewhere in the village, there was the sound of children desperately calling out from beneath the earth. Their stifled voices haunted his prison. Coming back again and again. Weeping . . . weeping.

Patu groaned and retreated into the deep folds of her robe. In the frail light of the little room, Sitko could see tears flowing from her troubled eyes.

"Every night since you came here, I hear much crying," she said. "Every night this crying comes from the place where the children are put until we understand what kind of creature you are. But the crying, it also comes from this room. A terrible, sad sound from this room where you stay. Like the sound of another child. And this crying all around me in the night, it makes me very sad, for I am a powerful woman who loves all the children. And all the children, they love Patu. But now, Patu is afraid. Patu is afraid for all the children."

"But they wouldn't kill children . . . certainly they wouldn't hurt the children," Sitko insisted.

"Yes, they will do it," Patu murmured, covering her face and groaning. "The children will die. And they will never be reborn clean and new into the first world. Pity us . . . pity us," Patu softly sobbed. "It is a bad day for us. It is a bad day for Patu. Delito, he wants your life. That much I know. I watch him, and I know he wants your life enough to throw away everything . . . even the lives of the children."

74

Sitko pressed his fingers to his forehead, trying to escape the panic that overtook him. Trying to convince himself that none of this could be happening. He groaned. He muttered without saying anything. He felt as if his brain were about to burst with an agony so great that it took complete possession of him. He stumbled to his feet, trying to escape the violent sensation that was taking over his body. He paced frantically from wall to wall of the little room. Again and again. He tried to think, but he could hear nothing but the sound of Patu sobbing. He could hear nothing but the weeping. That pitiable sound brought him to his knees. He fell to the ground in front of Patu and he embraced her, whispering comfort, trying to silence the terrible sound of weeping.

But Sitko could hear nothing but the sound of weeping. He covered his ears to the sound of people crying. But from behind the gray walls, he could hear nothing else but a long low lament.

He closed his eyes, he covered his ears, but still he heard the lament. Looking back into the darkness of his mind, Sitko could see the forlorn eyes of the children of Star of Good Hope as they vainly searched the darkness for their mothers and fathers. Looking back, he could see his mother leading him away. Looking back . . . looking back, he could see nothing but the tormented eyes of children . . . weeping. Even here and now, in this godforsaken place, he could hear still the desperate cry of those long-ago children of Star of Good Hope, their woeful voices merging with the everlasting sounds of weeping. Beyond the world, somewhere in the dark . . . everywhere . . . there was still the inconsolable howl of frightened children . . . weeping . . . weeping.

PART II: INITIATION

"THE PLAGUE"

The great plague is not made to human measure. You think therefore that the plague is unreal, it is a bad dream which will pass. . . . Our fellow citizens went on about their business. . . . How could they have thought of the plague which abolishes the future? They thought of themselves as free, but no one will ever be free as long as there are plagues.

—ALBERT CAMUS

NINE

IT WAS IN the time of the autumn fires that Sitko vowed he would survive. It was in the smoke-filled days of autumn that he became determined to ride upon adversity as a swimmer rides upon a wave, balancing precariously at its crest, high above the crushing underbelly of the furiously churning water. He soared above danger on the back of his art, covering the walls of his little room with pictures. He worked day and night. He worked and he waited. And while he waited, he planned for the next interrogation, when he would prove that he was not evil.

Moisture hung in the yellow air. The Sun was hidden by great clouds of smoke that for many days had tumbled over the desert, pushed relentlessly forward by the great forest fires in the distant mountains. The stench and fumes were so thick they burned Sitko's nostrils. Ash lingered in the windless sky. A meager light filtered through the smoke, turning the day into perpetual twilight. And Sitko sat on the ground, intently drawing pictures on every scrap of cardboard Patu brought to him, trying to occupy his thoughts, trying to stay alive. Covering the surfaces of walls and paper with the vivid images that tumbled down upon him from every day of his life.

In the evening he grappled in the failing light until he found another scrap of paper, and then, without opening his eyes, he scribbled until he had made the image of a man's face. All the lines collided, running rampantly into each other and piercing the angry grimace of that long-remembered face. The lines attacked the image, gouging out the cruel, little eyes, until at last the face lay dead beneath the sharp point of Sitko's charcoal stick.

Sitko gazed at the face he had destroyed, amazed by the rage he still felt for a man he barely remembered. And as he stared at the face, its lips began to move.

"Your father came to see me," the principal's face said. "He tells me that you're in a shell. Do you know what that means, Seymour Miller? He says that you don't have any friends, and that you work too hard at your studies and spend all the rest of your time making pictures."

Sitko continued to gaze at the face.

"I know that art is important to you," the face said. "And that's all very nice in its way. But you know, Seymour, there are other things in life besides pictures and books and school. You need to be a well-rounded fellow if you want to succeed in this life," the principal said without looking up from the papers on his desk. "Your adviser tells me you never attend school dances. You don't have any girlfriends. And the coach says that you constantly skip your physical education classes. I don't think I've ever seen you at a football game. . . ."

The principal paused. He looked at Sitko with an impatient expression on his face. "Do you understand what I'm talking about, Seymour? And if you do, why can't you speak up like a man?"

Sitko turned away. He did not dare look the man in the face, for surely if he did the principal would see the intense disgust that filled Sitko's eyes.

"Look at me when I'm talking to you, young man!" the principal shouted with growing anger. "Do you hear what I'm saying to you?"

"Yes, I understand!" Sitko muttered, glaring at the man's face, unable to restrain himself any longer. "Yes, I understand *exactly* what you are saying! But the problem is that you don't know what you're talking about! For one thing, Alexander Miller is not my father. And he's not married to my mother. If you really want to know the truth, he sleeps with my mother but he's not my mother's husband. He is not a nice man, and I don't give a damn what he thinks about me! What I do with my time is none of his business, and it's also none of your business!" Then Sitko smirked at the principal as his rage overflowed. "I'm going to get out of your goddam school! And I'm going to make something of myself! I'm going to art school! That's where I'm going! And, goddammit, one day I'm going to be a painter! Do you hear me? *I'm going to be a painter!* Not a wimp like you! And not an asshole like all the kids around here! So go ahead and talk all you want. You can't punish me because I paint pictures! And you can't punish me for not going to your idiotic football games!"

The principal leaped from his chair and grabbed Sitko.

"Who do you think you're talking to?" he shouted as he shook Sitko violently.

"Who do you think you're talking to, you little sonofabitch? I'll teach you how to talk to your elders!" And he slapped Sitko across the face. When Sitko didn't back away, the man's anger flared and he began beating Sitko with his fists.

Each time the principal struck him, Sitko saw in flashes everyone who had been unkind to him. He saw Alexander Milas-Miller, and he saw the headmaster of Star of Good Hope. He saw the ruins of his Chinese garden, and he saw the jeering faces of classmates. He also saw the expression of satisfaction that filled the principal's face as he hit him again and again with all his might. But he no longer felt pain, so great was the rage that filled him. He added each blow to all the other blows of his life. He added the pain to all the rest of the pain. When blood began to flow from Sitko's nose, the principal pushed him away and fell into his chair, staring at Sitko's battered face as if he did not believe what he had done. Sitko wiped the blood away with his sleeve. For a moment he stared at the principal. He wanted to remember his face. He wanted to remember that ugly face forever. Then he walked out of the office and slammed the door behind him.

The sound of the slamming door reverberated. Sitko could hear it again and again as he turned away from the drawing of the principal's slashed face. For a moment he clenched his teeth in rage, until suddenly he was startled by a noise.

"Who is it?" Sitko called. "Who is it?"

Someone was unlocking the door of his prison. He trembled as he anxiously peered through the smoke-filled room. The door opened slowly. Then Patu quietly entered, bringing a bowl of food. It was a great relief to see her. She was the only connection Sitko had with the world. She was the only person with whom he could talk. For no apparent reason, tears flowed into Sitko's eyes as he looked at Patu. He covered his face in shame and could not speak.

"You do not sleep. You do not eat," Patu said with a sigh of concern. "All you do is make more pictures. Always more pictures."

With a deep groan, she sat across from Sitko and placed the bowl of food on the ground between them. "I start thinking maybe it is true what you say. Maybe you truly are what you say. . . ."

"A painter . . . an artist," Sitko murmured. "An artist . . ." he repeated, wiping away his tears and concentrating on the sketch of another face he was drawing.

"Ahuh . . ." Patu whispered, craning her neck so she could see the face that Sitko had made. "That is a nice one . . . not like the terrible faces you always make. This one is a nice face. And who is this young man? Who is this young man whose face you have stolen?"

"This one . . ." Sitko said, looking intently at Patu, "this one is a face I won't see again. His name is Eric Jones."

"And what kind of name is that?"

"It's just a name," Sitko mused, as a grieved expression came into his eyes. "Now it's just a name."

Then he fell silent.

A spider twisted on its glowing thread, dangling upside down, moving its long back legs in an endless succession of meticulous gestures, conjuring silver out of nothing.

"And this face . . . it is perhaps your good friend," Patu questioned in a whisper.

The spider slowly twirled upon its silver thread, spiraling toward the ground. Its many legs undulated in the dimness of the smoky yellow light of a day that turned to night. It was on just such a moonlit night that Eric and Sitko had fallen asleep on the edge of a high-cut bank near the river. In deep summer. When the heat loomed just above the luminous earth, and every leaf and flower was intensely defined and real. The moonlight lingered tangibly in the humid air. And the turbulent river seemed strangely motionless, as if it were held captive by the Moon.

The spider twisted from a branch on its glowing thread. An owl hooted in the distance, and Sitko trembled.

"What's the matter?" Eric Jones asked.

"That sound is the voice of someone who is dead," Sitko whispered. "It is a bad sign. My grandmother used to say that some dead man was turned into an owl and had to live forever in the night, deprived of the Sun."

A wolf howled. A long, sorrowful sound.

"Ah," Sitko sighed. "That is so sad. It sounds as if the wolf has lost something very precious. Do you think he will ever find it again?"

Eric did not respond.

Sitko pondered the smoke that ringed the yellow Moon. The river resounded all around. The rapids roared, but their cascades were frozen in the moonlight. Nothing moved. Yet everything had a sound and a scent—the wolf, the rocks, the stars.

Leaf patterns fell upon them, speckling Eric's body with shadows.

He turned lazily, facing Sitko, and the image of the branches wove an ornamental net across his dark thighs.

"Will you take off your clothes?" Eric whispered.

Sitko smiled slowly as he unfastened his shirt, and he laughed as he climbed out of his pants.

"And will you take off your necklace?"

Sitko hesitated, touching the turquoise stones that always hung around his neck. Then he shook his head apologetically.

"Not the necklace. The necklace is from my grandmother . . . I must keep the necklace."

"Why keep it? It's only a few stones. You'd make me very happy if you'd let me wear your necklace," Eric said, smiling.

"It is something I must keep for myself," Sitko said softly. "We must all keep something for ourselves. That is what I have learned from my grandmother Amana. We must have ourselves and we must also have a people to whom we belong . . . a people with a belief in us . . . a people who know that we exist." And then Sitko paused, and a sad look came over his dark face. "It's terrible not to have a people. It is terrible to be abandoned, to be cast out and forgotten. And so, do you see, I must keep this one thing that reminds me of those faraway days of my people, or nothing will remain of them."

The wolf howled and Sitko sighed. He began to speak again, but Eric put his hand to his lips. Slowly they retreated into each other, limb upon limb. As they enfolded each other, their bodies smelled like berries and horses. And then they rolled slowly into the deep, wet grass, while the night was perfectly white in the moonlight.

They came together hesitantly, filling the space between them slowly, until the Moon disappeared behind their eyes and the grass began to sing its long green song. Even the spider vanished from the air, leaving nothing but a luminous silver trellis.

The night stretched out in the moonlight, arching its back where the mountains rose and sending up mist where the river tumbled moment by moment into the dark valley.

"And this face . . ." Patu said, as she gazed at an image on the gray walls of the prison.

Sitko ran his fingers over the cheek of the face he had drawn on the wall.

"Reno . . . his name is Reno. This one is my brother, Reno."

"Ayh . . . so this is Reno. Ayh, this Reno, he has a nice face. But it is sad. Why is your brother Reno's face so sad?"

"I don't know," Sitko muttered, looking harder at the image on the wall, trying to fathom its pained expression. "I always thought he was the strong one. I thought he was the lucky one. I always thought he was happy, and I was the one who was confused. But when he was drinking he used to get depressed. We didn't talk much in those days, except when he was drinking. Then he talked his head off. I remember one night when I was still in high school. I wanted to talk to him. But his car wasn't in the garage, so I knew he was out drinking."

Jemina had already gone upstairs for the night. And Alexander Miller sat silently in his big chair in the den, his arms crossed over his belly as he stared vacantly into space. Sitko peered at his foster father in silence, hoping to creep past the door without being noticed.

Once Alexander Milas-Miller had been an aerialist. Sitko had seen the photograph albums in the attic. Alexander wore white tights and a glittering, sequined bolero. Together Alexander Milas and Jamie Ghost Horse had flown through the air like glistening birds. In the photographs, Alexander and Jamie were still fine-looking youths—frozen forever on faded sepia cardboard. Looking marvelous in their costumes. Their strong bodies poised for flight. Smiling wildly at one another and embracing with the extraordinary comradery of two young bullfighters about to enter the ring.

But now the circus was gone. Jamie was gone. And Alexander Miller was no longer built for the air. Now his face was puffy, and the handsome young man in the faded photographs had vanished under years and years of wrinkles and fat. He no longer had a bushy mustache, and his hair was falling out, leaving a nakedness to his face that made him look like a strange, overgrown infant. Now he sat silently in his big chair. Night after night he dozed in his chair, watching something in the air that no one else could see. And when he fell asleep, a trace of saliva would slowly ooze down his chins.

Sitko backed away from the dozing Alexander and went to Reno's room. He was determined to sit up until Reno came home, but he was so exhausted that he eventually climbed into the bed without getting undressed. He put a pillow over his head and fell asleep. But he could not escape himself, even in his dreams. He heard Jemina and Alexander Miller yelling at one another, and he saw himself running to the closet where the rifle was kept. He grabbed the gun and rushed into the living room, just as Alexander was strangling his mother. He shouted as he pointed the rifle at Alexander's head. Then he fired. He fired again. The shots burst in the air. Blood spouted upward in a crimson storm, blinding Sitko . . . drenching his groin. When he tried to cry out, the world vanished. He groaned in his sleep, and tears welled up in his closed eyes.

Sitko awoke with a start. Reno was sitting on the edge of the bed, smiling down at him.

He was drunk.

"You were having one hell of a nightmare, asshole," Reno stammered as he stroked Sitko's head. "You're still such a little kid. Still afraid of the fucking dark."

Sitko pulled the covers over his head.

"Still afraid of the goddam bogeyman," Reno giggled as he playfully jabbed at Sitko's ribs.

"Come on, Reno, give it a rest. I need to talk to you, and you're drunk. Isn't that just great!" Sitko complained.

"What's that supposed to mean?" Reno growled defensively. "What the fuck is that snide remark supposed to mean? Here I'm trying to be nice to you 'cause you were yelling bloody murder in your sleep and a lot of thanks I get!"

"Reno . . ." Sitko whispered, putting his finger to his lips, "have a heart. The old man is just looking for an excuse to have a fight with me. So be quiet and listen to what I have to say."

"Fuck you . . ." Reno muttered, pushing his brother's hand away.

"Come on, Reno. Listen to what I'm saying," Sitko pleaded. "I've got to talk to you."

"I don't give a shit!"

"Please, Reno, have a heart. It's important."

"All right . . . all right . . . so talk."

"I've decided to quit school.

"Are you out of your fucking mind?" Reno exclaimed. "What do you mean, you're quitting school? What the hell are you talking about?"

"Listen to me, Reno . . . I've got to get away from here while I'm still sane. If I stick around here I'll never amount to anything. Alexander hates everything I do and say, and Mother just goes along with him. I've got to pack it in and get out on my own. That's the only way I'll ever get to art school."

"No . . . no . . . no," Reno said with drunken concern, trying to focus his thoughts. "You can't do that, asshole. You don't even have a pot to piss in, for chrissake!"

"I got a scholarship. . . ."

"Big fucking deal! And where will that get you? Look, kid, I gotta talk to you, 'cause that's a really dumb idea. I'm the one . . . that's right, me. I'm the one that's got to get out of here. But you . . . you got talent, and so you just stop all this bullshit. You got to finish school and make something of yourself," he stammered, fishing for something in his pockets that he couldn't find. "Do you hear what I'm telling you?"

"Okay . . . okay . . . we'll talk later," Sitko said, realizing that his brother was in no condition to talk. "It's late. So maybe we should wait till tomorrow to talk about it."

"Don't give me that crap! I want to talk about it *now!*" Reno shouted.

"Okay . . . okay . . . but not so loud."

Reno blinked dazedly into Sitko's face, putting his hands on each side of his head and drawing him close. "Now listen to me, little brother," he demanded, "no more nonsense about quitting school! You hear? No more nonsense! Or you're gonna break my heart. . . ." As he said this, Reno's shoulders slouched and he shook his head wearily as he began to sob.

"I've had a terrible night," he mumbled. "A terrible night! Goddammit, I've had a terrible time of it. This life is shit! Do you know that? It's shit, and I'm ready to quit. That's how bad it is."

Sitko was dumbfounded. He sat up in bed and looked

helplessly at his brother, not knowing how to comfort him. He had never seen Reno behave like this. Even when he was drinking, Reno never let anyone see his feelings.

"Jesus . . ." Reno wept. "What a mess! Our lousy father is somewhere out there . . . who knows where! Drunk! He's always fucking drunk . . . just like me. Like father, like miserable son! And Grandma Amana has lost her marbles! Old and half crazy! And Mother's whoring it up with that Greek sonofabitch Alexander. And look at you! My little brother is some kind of weirdo. And me—I'm a goddam alcoholic! Jesus, what a mess!"

"Come on, Reno," Sitko murmured as he embraced his brother. "We can't all fall apart. You've got to be the strong one. Pull yourself together."

"I don't even know what the hell I'm talking about, and tomorrow I'll go right back to my fucking job and deny every word of this. But right now . . . right now, goddammit, it hurts like hell just to be alive. And you're the only one who understands or cares about me." Reno sobbed uncontrollably.

"It's going to be okay," Sitko promised, feeling wave upon wave of desperation rolling like a tidal wave over the house of Alexander Milas-Miller. "Come on, I'll help you get into bed, and tomorrow when you feel better we can talk about all of this. Okay?"

"No," Reno pleaded, clinging to Sitko. "Don't go! Everybody is always going away. I want you to stay here for a while, Sy. I need you to stay here with me for a little while or I don't think I can make it. I tell you, I'm not gonna make it," he panted as he stretched out next to Sitko and closed his eyes.

They lay in the darkness for a long time. Then Sitko felt

his brother's body trembling as he began to weep again.

"Jesus, Reno, what's the matter with you?" he murmured. "What's happening to you?"

"I'm losing it. That's what's happening to me. I'm fucking losing it! I'm never gonna amount to anything. I don't have any talent. I've just made a mess out of everything."

"Come on," Sitko gently urged, putting his arms around his brother. "It's not all that bad. You're plenty smart. And you've got a great job, and you've got great looks and personality. Hell, Reno, everybody always likes you."

"It's all fake," he sobbed. "It's just a pack of lies."

Sitko hugged his brother and tried to comfort him. But nothing seemed to help. Reno buried his face against Sitko's chest and shook with sobs.

Then suddenly the door to the bedroom flew open and the lights went on, blinding Sitko. He sat up in terror, not knowing what was happening.

Alexander Miller stood in the doorway, shaking with rage.

"What the hell is going on in here?" he shouted. "My God, what has been going on in this house?"

Sitko stumbled out of bed and tried to pull his brother to his feet. He was half conscious, and even Alexander's outburst did not rouse him.

"I want both of you out of this house! Now! Right now! I want you out of here!" Alexander shouted again and again. "I want you perverted faggot bastards out of my house tonight!"

"He's drunk," Sitko exclaimed, dragging his brother out of Alexander's frenzied reach. "What the hell's the matter with you? For chrissake, he's just drunk!"

"What were you two doing in here in the dark this time

of night? That's what I want to know! What were you faggot bastards doing in here?" Alexander shouted as Jemina rushed into the bedroom and tried to calm him. "I'll kill them! I'll kill the both of you! I'll put a bullet in both their faggot heads!" he roared as he snatched at them and Jemina restrained him.

"*Please!*" Jemina cried, as she tried to hold him back. "They're brothers, for godsake! What are you thinking? They're just brothers!"

"Brothers my ass! I know what they are! And I want both of them out of here!" Alexander yelled again and again, panting as if he had gone mad and straining against Jemina's grasp, snatching out at the brothers. "I want both of them out of this house right now!"

"Please listen to me," Jemina pleaded.

"No! No more listening to you! I don't want to hear it! I just want your lousy sons out of here!" Alexander bellowed, as he tore himself free and started for the hallway. "If they're still here when I get back, I swear to God I'm gonna blow their goddam brains out!"

"My God! He's going for the rifle!" Jemina screamed, frantic with fear. She pushed Sitko aside and ran to Reno, who was passed out on his bed. "You've got to get out of here before he kills everybody!" she cried. "Sitko," she wailed, "you're so young—he'll forgive you! But you've got to help me get your brother out of here before he comes back!"

While Jemina wept, Sitko slapped and shook Reno until he awoke, and then Jemina helped drag him downstairs and into the kitchen. All the while they could hear Alexander Miller frantically banging closet doors as he searched for his rifle.

"My God . . . oh, my God! Hurry, please hurry, Sitko!

Hurry! We've got to get the two of you out of here!"

By the time Sitko had dragged his brother halfway down the hall, he could see Alexander standing at the head of the stairs. A violent blast exploded in Sitko's ears.

"My God, you've killed them! You've killed them!" Sitko could hear his mother screaming as he pulled Reno toward Grandma Amana's room.

The old woman rushed out when she heard Sitko shouting for help. Instantly she understood what had to be done. An immense power lighted her face as she placed her hands upon the brothers' bodies, making certain they were not injured. Then she whirled about like a warrior and, with a piercing shout, she ran into the pantry. In a moment she returned, wide-eyed, clutching a knife.

"No one will harm you!" she muttered fiercely. "As long as I'm alive nobody is going to hurt you!"

Reno moaned as Sitko took his face in both his hands and peered into his confused eyes. "Can you understand what I'm telling you, Reno?" Sitko shouted. "Reno, we've got to get the hell out of here right now. The old man has gone crazy! Everything will be okay tomorrow, but right now we've got to get out of here!"

Without really understanding what was happening, Reno blinked at Sitko and then, with his arms wheeling, he staggered outside after his brother, down the walk, out the front gate, and into the night.

Now nothing remains but a cascade of fantastic images that pour from the fingers of Sitko Ghost Horse. The past begs to be remembered in his strong colors. He is the keeper of the hours and the days. They cry out from his paintings. The people and the names continue to live in his pictures. They are alive in his fingers as the darkness begins to come down.

The great house of Alexander Milas-Miller stands against the evening sky. The day is ending in a perpetual flood of moths. Nothing moves over the grass or around the tennis courts. The trees are fixed for a moment against the diminishing sky. And the wind stops to catch its breath.

The windows of this great house are closed and dark now. No one can enter or leave. Now there are no lights, no radios, no angry voices. Everyone has left this solemn house of broken dreams to face the night alone.

"And this face . . ." came Patu's voice, speaking to him from a great distance. "And this face . . ." Patu was saying, as she gazed at the image on the wall.

Sitko gently ran his fingers over the face. "Reno," he murmured sadly. "His name was Reno."

"It is a nice face . . . but a sad face. Why is the face so sad?"

Sitko looked hard at the image on the wall, trying to fathom its pained expression. "I don't know . . ." he said with confusion. "I really don't know. I always thought he was happy. I always thought he had everything I lacked. I used to feel guilty because I envied him so much. But I guess all along he envied me. God knows why. And you know, in a sad sort of way, all of that is rather funny."

The paint on the shutters is beginning to crack and splinter. The lock that holds the front door aches with rust and the stiffness of old age.

There are no butterflies in the oak trees, and birds no longer visit this forlorn house of Alexander Milas-Miller.

The blue-and-white morning glories have begun their nightly retreat. They will not bloom again. The grass has turned gray. And the night collects itself into deep shadows among the bushes where the smudged footprints of Jamie Ghost Horse have filled with rain, though they can never entirely vanish from memory.

T E N

IT WAS ON the day of the second interrogation that the pain returned to Sitko's leg. When he opened his eyes he found that his leg was swollen and ached so horribly that he could barely clutch at consciousness. He could not sit up, and yet he knew that he could not remain helpless on the floor.

"Someone please help me! You out there, can you hear me? Please do not leave me in here without help!"

After a long pause, the bolt moved and the door was opened just slightly. Two eyes peered in at him. For just a moment the person at the door hesitated and Sitko's hope rose. But then the door snapped shut.

"Ah," Sitko groaned.

The pain in his leg was so terrible that he felt dizzy. When he summoned a great effort and managed to sit up he discovered a stout stick which he thought he might use as a cane. But the pain pierced his back and leg, and no amount of effort and endurance could get him to his feet.

Somehow his injured leg, which had seemed greatly improved, was badly discolored and swollen. Surely it would only get worse without treatment. Patu was his only hope for help, but Sitko had no idea how long it would be before she came to his prison. The pain was steadily increasing, the swelling was much worse, and Sitko was frightened.

That was when he realized that someone had been sitting just behind him all this time. It was the man called Delito.

Sitko cried out in surprise when he discovered this fearsome man sitting there. He had never seen him at close proximity. And he was fascinated by his face. The man was extremely ugly—much uglier than Sitko had realized. His flabby belly protruded over his hips and sides. Flesh hung limply from his arms. His skin was gray and pitted. And his breath stank. He sat silently, blinking his little gray eyes and staring blankly at Sitko.

For a long time they did not speak. Delito simply looked at Sitko. Like a vulture gazing at a dying calf. It seemed to Sitko that Delito had absolutely no intention of doing anything but stare at him. Perhaps he had been there the entire night, leaning over Sitko and watching him while he slept, counting his heartbeats, sniffing at his face like a cat hovering over a sleeping child. For all Sitko knew he might have done some mischief to his leg, and was lingering in the hope that Sitko would die while he silently watched.

Sitko detested this ugly man, but he was at his mercy. "Please help me," Sitko pleaded, hoping Delito would not turn away at the first sound of his voice. Instead, he did nothing. He simply continued to stare blankly at Sitko.

"Please help me," Sitko urged, as the pain grew worse and he feared he might faint. But Delito said nothing. He sat on the ground and peered intently at Sitko's face and swollen leg, slowly twisting one of his hands inside the other.

With each twist of his hand, the throbbing intensified in Sitko's leg. Sitko's face screwed up with pain. Delito leaned close and gazed into the tormented face. And very slowly a faint smile lighted his dreadful, empty eyes.

Finally he spoke. "Tell me, stranger, what are you doing here? Are you a fool or a wise man? Are you good or are you evil?"

Sitko drew a breath and was about to try to give the man some kind of answer.

"No!" Delito snapped. "Do not tell me! Let me guess!"

With this, Delito laughed as he got up on his short little legs and stared aimlessly into Sitko's pain-racked face.

"Let me see . . . let me see," he said with a smirk. "Surely you must be a fool, because you cannot get up. There seems to be something terribly wrong with your leg."

"Yes . . ." Sitko murmured in shame, as he realized that Delito was delighting in abusing him.

"And let me see . . ." Delito continued, "you must be evil, because I don't like your eyes. And I don't like the way you look. And I don't like the way you talk!"

"I'm in terrible pain. You must help me! I cannot move!"

"Help yourself," the ugly little man cackled, as he turned toward the door to leave.

"No! Please don't go away!"

"And why should I stay? Are you going to do something amusing?" Delito said with a giggle, a trace of blood flowing from his nostrils. "Of course, if you are going to dance on that leg, then certainly I wouldn't miss it for the world. But if all you plan to do is complain, well, then, I really don't want to stay here." And again he turned to leave.

"Please! I don't know what I've done! I'm sorry if I have done something wrong. I really don't know why you hate me. And I apologize if I've done something I shouldn't have done!"

Delito laughed unpleasantly. "You *apologize* . . ." he hissed under his breath, his eyes glowing and red as his motley hair spread like cobwebs over his face. "You *apologize!*"

Delito gritted his fierce little teeth and shouted as he twisted one of his hands inside the other. At once Sitko screamed with pain and fell to the ground panting.

Sitko tried to swallow. He tried to moisten his lips so he could speak despite the overwhelming pain that welled up in his leg like a vast and terrible toothache. He threw back his head in agony and tried desperately to remain conscious, for he knew if he passed out and Delito left him, he would not survive.

"Poor boy," Delito whispered with a leer. "Well, then, perhaps you should do exactly what I tell you to do."

And he laughed as he walked slowly around Sitko and inspected him carefully.

"Perhaps if you obey me, you will be all right after all," he said, squatting next to Sitko and sniffing at him several times. Then he grabbed Sitko by the hair and pulled his head far back and looked into Sitko's half-closed eyes.

Sitko panted in shame and fear. He tried to nod his head to the man. To give some kind of response that wouldn't anger him. He gasped for breath and swallowed again and again, still trying to moisten his parched mouth so he could speak.

With an expression of disgust and petulance, Delito abruptly released Sitko's head. Immediately the pain in Sitko's leg began to subside.

"Thank you . . ." Sitko groaned with relief.

But Delito said nothing. He sat beside Sitko with an aimless smile on his ugly face. His blank little eyes rolled aimlessly in his head.

When Sitko had gathered enough strength to speak, he asked, "What must I do? What must I do to be set free?"

Delito gave Sitko a contemptuous look. "You smell bad. You smell very bad. But I could use you. I can use you very nicely, but only if you promise to do just as I say."

"What must I do?"

"At the meeting . . . in the chamber . . . you will tell them that you are a liar and a thief and an abomination. You will tell them that you came here to bring sickness and evil. That is what you must do!"

Sitko was silent. If he was to live, he needed Delito's help. He did not want to have anything to do with him. He wanted to escape. He wanted to go back to the city he had fled.

"Are you listening? I said I will save your life," Delito shouted, staring intently at Sitko, "but you must promise to take care of me in return!"

For a long time Sitko remained silent. Then, at last, he nodded.

"But do you promise?" Delito shouted. "I want your promise to do exactly what I tell you to do!"

"Yes . . . yes, I promise."

"I'm happy to hear that. Soon I will be leaving you. But when we meet again, your time will be up."

"And will you divulge your secrets?"

"I have no secrets."

"So you know nothing."

"I have nothing to tell," Delito whispered with a vicious smile. Then he laughed and hopped onto his little legs and hurried toward the door. The sweet odor of decay flew into the wind and followed after him. An obedient shadow trailed doggedly in his footsteps. And as he moved through the door, he left a fragile trail of cinders and blood. Then he vanished.

When Delito returned he brought water in one gourd and dried leaves in another. Then Delito settled down on the ground next to Sitko. He winked incessantly and moved his purple tongue over his lips as he soaked the herbs in water. Then he spread the compress over Sitko's swollen leg and bound it with strips of soft hide. "Now, you will be healed," he said. "Do you see how easy it is when you know the secret of life and death? Do you begin to understand my power, Goat-Boy?"

"My name is not Goat-Boy," Sitko said sullenly, looking away in shame.

"I know that!" snapped Delito. "It is Sitko or Seymour or something or other, depending on the time of day. Yes, I know all about you. That is why you are afraid of me. I know things that no one else knows. I know that just under your flesh you still have a little scar on that beautiful face of yours. Yes, I know about the scar. And I know about many other things! I know that you are already thinking what you can do to escape me, even though I am saving your miserable life!" With this, Delito laughed and spit on Sitko's leg.

At that moment, the door opened and Patu came into the room. She acted as if she did not notice that Delito was there, though he shouted something at her and raised his arms in some ritual of protection, trying to keep her away. But Patu strode forward and pushed the man out of her way. She stood over Sitko. When Delito began to object, she waved him away with a gesture, and he fell back in fear.

Patu dropped to her knees and a great torrent of grief seized her and many tears fell from her eyes.

"Ah," she wailed, "the world of his heart is already dark and night waits like a wolf for him to lay down his life. Flowers bend heavily on their stems. Everything wishes to sleep, but you must wake up. Do you hear me? Listen to the wind in the trees. There is life in the trees. You must awaken now. For this dream will surely kill you. Wake up and do not be afraid. I will find the poison in your leg and I will cut it out."

Patu shaded her eyes with a feather and peered at Sitko's swollen leg. "There it is! I can see it!" Now she began brushing the swollen flesh with the feather, gathering the saliva Delito had spat on the wound and pushing it into one terrible black sore just under the skin of Sitko's calf. Then she took out her knife and carefully cut into the evil. "I have it! I have it!"

The pain was fierce. Sitko cried out. But no sound came from his mouth.

Patu shook her head slowly and held out her hand so Sitko could see what was in her palm. There was a tiny knot of tangled black hair, like the motley hair on Delito's head. Sitko pulled away in repulsion. He felt sick. His head ached and he began to fall backward into the soft earth. He screamed in fear and pain. Plunging downward. Falling and falling. Silver falling. Red and crimson and turquoise falling. One million bells! One million claps of thunder! And he collapsed into the arms of the golden Sun, whose mouth was filled with corn silk. Sitko cried out again, but it was too late. The darkness had already taken possession of his eyes.

"Are you all right?" Patu cried out anxiously again and again. "Are you all right?"

When Sitko opened his eyes he saw an enormous Moon moving through the dark sky. It was the face of Patu. Her features gradually took shape in the darkness behind his eyes. Then she leaned slightly forward and she whispered, "Tell me, Artist, what is it that you saw? Tell me . . . what did you learn?"

Sitko anxiously stared into Patu's face, as he urgently grasped her extended hand. "What is happening to me?" he muttered distractedly.

"There is no time. We must hurry," Patu said. "I must take you to the meeting chamber. Hurry . . ."

"I don't think I can stand," Sitko sobbed, as he tried to get to his feet.

"Why can you not stand? What is the matter?"

"I don't think I can . . ." Sitko began, only to discover that he could easily rise to his feet. He took a few hesitant steps. There was no pain. No swelling. Nothing at all. In astonishment he gaped at Patu, but she paid no attention.

"Hurry . . . I must take you now."

They quickly left the prison and made their way through the yellow cloud that hung over the desert. Hundreds of buzzards screamed at them, dancing from foot to foot and spreading their wide wings threateningly as Sitko and Patu made their way through heaps of decomposing carcasses. The stench was overpowering, and Sitko covered his face and tried to rest. But Patu urged him onward. When they emerged from the yellow mist, Sitko found himself in a field of burned-out tree trunks that stood forlornly against the blazing sky. Everywhere were piles of discarded tires, refrigerators, air conditioners, and the wrecks of countless automobiles, dismembered and rusted, their windows shattered and splintered like cobwebs. An enormous cargo truck lay on its side, its eighteen wheels spinning helplessly in the air. Two little boys clamored noisily on top of the upended vehicle, running the full length of its aluminum siding and then squatting at the edge and peering intently down at Sitko as he and Patu hurried past. Then the drumming began in the distance. Patu limped faster and faster, despite her withered leg. Sitko could barely keep up with her gigantic strides. They splashed through a deep wallow afloat with beer cans and surgical refuse. Everything was covered with a thick coating of pitch. On the other side of the wallow was a little house. A starving dog with only three legs hobbled past them, chased by a blind child with a knife. Six emaciated, featherless roosters crowded on top of the open door of the house, whose roof had collapsed and whose walls were charred by fire. A large bed was still ablaze within the house, and its raging flames were encircled by a dense flock of thousands upon thousands of moths, whose wings crackled noisily in the fire.

They crossed a field of broken glass. Then they climbed a wall and pushed into a grove of tall dead grass, which caught in their hair and restrained them like a thorny net. Sitko and Patu staggered forward. The distance between them and the meeting chamber seemed to grow with each step they took. Finally, they climbed a knoll and descended into the dusky landscape surrounding the meeting place. They rushed up a succession of twisting stairways that led to the center of the village.

"We are here!" Patu exclaimed with relief.

Sitko leaned forward, trying to catch his breath.

"Now, listen before we go inside," Patu said. "It is important," she told him, "for you to be wise. Do not anger Delito. He wants you to do just that. It makes him feel happy when you are angry. It will make people think maybe he is right about you. So try very hard to be wise and quiet. Otherwise Delito will say you are evil."

"I don't care about him," Sitko whispered. "What I need to know is what you think."

Patu hesitated.

"Please," he whispered.

She looked into the distance as if she expected to find an answer there. Still she remained silent. Then she turned to him and said, "I cannot tell you what you ask. And I cannot tell you why." And she was silent for a moment. At length, she looked intently at Sitko. "Forgive me, but I cannot. Even when I hear your voice and when I see the pictures you make, still there is something that I cannot find in you. I do not know exactly what it is, but I know that it is not there. This thing that you do not have . . . I believe that long ago you had this thing . . . but now it is gone. You are kind and you are beautiful and you have the power to make strong pictures, but there is something else I look for in you, and I cannot find it. When you dream, you do not dream of this land, but of another place. And when I hear you singing, it is not our song that you sing. When I search for you in the dark, I find nothing familiar. I cannot see what it is I am looking for. I only catch glimpses of someone in the distance. A face in the smoke. A voice in the silence of the morning. But as the days go by I grow weary of trying to find you. I have searched into your face for so long and I have found nothing I understand. I do not believe that you are evil. But I do not know if you are good. I cannot find myself among your thoughts and your pictures. And I cannot say to you what you want to hear, and I cannot tell you why. But if I try to explain, I too will lose what it is that you have lost. Forgive me, my friend, but I cannot lose such a precious thing. I cannot lose it. And so, forgive me, but I cannot tell you what you ask of me."

Sitko lowered his head and sighed. He wanted to respond, but there was nothing for him to say. After a moment, he looked at Patu with both affection and dismay.

For the very first time she smiled. It was a shy smile that hesitated again and again and almost didn't happen. Then, in a moment, it was gone.

"The meeting chamber . . ." Patu said quietly. "Now it is time for the meeting chamber."

ELEVEN

▲

"YOU SAY THAT you are not a housepainter," Delito declared officiously, as he meandered through the chamber, an expression of delighted derision on his face.

"That is correct. I am not a housepainter. I am an artist."

"And is there any difference?"

Sitko laughed quietly, but dared not express what he felt. He simply answered: "Yes."

"And what is the difference?"

"That is a difficult question to answer because it is not a good question," Sitko said flatly. "If you had seen a painting you could not ask such a question."

"Ah . . ." Delito slyly murmured. "But we have seen what you call *painting*. Is that not true?" he asked the assembly. "Have we not seen the filth this stranger has made on the walls of his room?"

The elders on the right mumbled their affirmation, while the people on the left made a great deal of noise that seemed neither to agree nor to disagree with Delito's statement.

With a gesture Delito silenced the audience and continued. "Sometimes when children misbehave they make such scribbling on walls. For this they are punished. But you tell us that the people in your world give you money for marking up the walls. Surely that is a lie. It cannot be true. It is unbelievable just as all that you say is unbelievable. Everything you claim to be the truth is a lie. If you were truly what you say you are . . . if you were what you call *a painter* . . . you wouldn't make a mess on walls like a mischievous child. You would paint a house!"

The people on the left burst into laughter, and Delito leered at Sitko with triumphant satisfaction.

"You don't understand what art is!" Sitko shouted over the noise.

"You are right!" Delito exclaimed. "But we know how to paint a house! And that is something you cannot do, because you are not one of us and because you are evil!"

Sitko threw up his hands in frustration.

"We have seen this *painting* of yours," Delito hissed in contempt. "And it is as evil as you are. You steal the spirits of people. You steal their faces and their bodies! We have seen how you do this! And you cannot deny it! You make people prisoners on walls and on pieces of cardboard. What purpose is there in such obscene magic? Only an evil purpose! There can be no other purpose!"

"That is ridiculous!" Sitko shouted over the uproar of the people on the left, who seemed completely persuaded by Delito's argument. "Paintings don't hurt anybody! Why are you afraid of them? How can you call pictures evil? How can you call my paintings obscene if you don't understand what they are? Please, believe me, my paintings are not evil. They are only shadows made of color. But they are my dreams. Without my paintings I am not fully human. I cannot exist without them. They keep me alive. And they also keep other people alive. There isn't a single place on earth where people don't make some kind of pictures!"

"Stop! Stop!" Delito shouted angrily. "That is clearly a lie," he proclaimed. "For we have no such people here! And we do not want any such people!"

Sitko tried to respond, but the noise in the meeting chamber was deafening. At length, Delito raised his arms to silence the raucous people on the left.

"Here, in this village . . ." Delito pronounced, "in this village things are good. This we know. Everywhere else is evil. That too we know. From *out there* comes disease that kills. From *out there* come men who steal the spirits of the land. From *out there* come terrible women whose vaginas have sharp teeth and whose children are born dead. From *out there* come evil people. People without names. People without families or clans! People without spirit! You are such a person! And this we know!"

"I have told you! I have already told you! I do have a name! I do have a family! And I am not evil!" Sitko protested.

"Then tell us! Who are you?"

"My name is Sitko Ghost Horse."

"Ha!" Delito shouted as he raised both his arms. "Is that who you really are?"

"Yes, Sitko Ghost Horse."

"Nonsense! What does such a ridiculous name mean?"

"It is just a name. It doesn't mean anything!"

"Ridiculous!" Delito shrieked. "It doesn't mean anything because it is a lie. It is a name you made up! That is what it is! If you were not an evil monster you would have a family that would give you a proper name that honors you! Not a foolish name! But you have no family because you were not born as we are born. You are not one of us! You are from *out there*!"

"That is not true!" Sitko objected again and again. "It is not true!"

"Then tell us, where do you come from? And who are your people?"

"My name is Sitko Ghost Horse! I don't know where I come from. I don't know where I was born! I was taken away from my people when I was still a child."

"Ha! Just as I said. You were not born as we are born! Because you are an evil thing that comes out of the slime of the swamp. Like a disease. Like a sickness that lives in the mud!"

"Of course I was born! I am the same as you. I am a person like you . . . like all of you. I am not what you say I am! You must listen to what I say! You must believe me!"

"Can you prove who you are?"

"How can anyone prove such a thing? Why can't you just believe what I have told you?"

"We will believe you when you tell us the truth! Not lies! Tell us! Where do you come from and who are your people?"

"I told you . . . my grandmother was called Amana! Her husband was Far Away Son! But he died. She had a child. With a stranger named Jean Pierre Bonneville! That child was my mother, Jemina Bonneville! And my father was called Jamie Ghost Horse! And my foster father was named Alexander Milas-Miller. They used to call me Seymour Miller. But I am really Sitko Ghost Horse! That is who I am! Why can't you just believe what I am telling you?"

Delito waved Sitko aside with a gesture of contempt and impatience. This action delighted the crowd, and there was a great burst of laughter.

"What you say is clearly a lie," Delito said without looking at Sitko. "Where are these people you name? And if they exist, why haven't they come here looking for you? If you have a family and friends, why haven't they come in search of you?"

"Because . . ." Sitko murmured, "because they are gone."

"Speak up! Speak up!"

"Because they are gone. . . ."

"What is this? Is there no one who will speak in your behalf? Is that what you tell us? That there is no one in your whole evil world who is willing to defend you?"

"No one . . ." Sitko whispered.

"No family? No friend? Aha! No one! Now, at last, we hear the truth! For it is said that evil people are without spirit . . . without name . . . without family or friend!" Delito shouted into Sitko's face.

"No one . . . no one . . ." Sitko whispered again and again. "No one is left. They are gone. Everyone is gone. I watched as they vanished, one by one. At first I thought I was fortunate. I thought I was incredibly lucky, because I was one of the few who survived. But then I realized something. I realized that it is more horrible to survive than it is to die. It is such agony to be alive in a world that is dying. Because you have to watch and listen. Because you always stand at a distance, watching as people are devoured. As their bodies

111

shrivel away to nothing. As their faces turn to pale bone and their eyes sink deeper and deeper into their black sockets. It is worse to be a witness than it is to be a victim. Because you must watch. Because you must listen. Day and night. Every-where. Hearing their inconsolable cries. Like the endless shriek of tormented cats. A shrill whine that goes on and on. The outcry of their inexpressible misery! On and on!''

The meeting chamber was silent. Everyone gazed at Sitko, wondering if perhaps there might be some element of truth in the sad things he was saying. But Delito would not permit their indecision. With a leer, he remarked to the crowd: "Very touching. Such a performance! But utter nonsense! This sad story of his would be touching if a word of it were true! But it is nothing but lies and more lies!''

"You must believe me!" Sitko shouted. "My grandmother was called Amana! Her husband was Far Away Son! My mother was Jemina Bonneville! And my father was Jamie Ghost Horse! My brother was named Reno! Those were my people! But now they are gone! Now all of them are gone! But they were my people! If they were alive they would speak in my behalf! They would defend me! They would save me! They would come in search of me! Because they loved me! And they were my people! I would not be here, if they were alive! I would be in the city with Eric! I would be painting! And I would not be in this terrible place!''

"This *terrible place*? Is that what you say?" Delito muttered sarcastically. "This *terrible place*. Then why did you come here? No one asked you to come here. You invaded our world! You came uninvited! Out of the slime! To exploit us! To bring sickness and death!''

"That is not true. It was an accident! I did not know where

I was going! I came here by accident! But however I got here, I have done nothing wrong. I will do whatever you want me to do," Sitko pleaded, "I will tell you whatever you want to know. But, believe me, I have done nothing wrong!"

From the back of the chamber came Patu's familiar voice. "Who is the person you call Eric? Tell us about this man named Eric," she urged.

Sitko searched the crowd for Patu's face. He needed the reassurance of her familiar face. But he could not find her in the crowd. He tried to compose himself, but he could not stop trembling. "Eric . . ." he murmured. "Eric Jones," he said. But his voice broke off, and unexpectedly tears began to flow from his eyes as his voice vanished into his chest.

"Tell us about Eric Jones," Patu's voice called out. "Tell us about your friend."

"Eric Jones . . ." he wept, unable to speak.

"Tell us about Eric Jones," a man on the right called out. "Tell us about him."

"My friend . . ." Sitko mumbled, wiping away his tears. "He was my friend. For many years. A writer . . . he was a writer. He wrote and I painted. In our studio. Music . . . there was always music in our studio. And people . . . friends . . . there were many friends. He was tall . . . Eric Jones. Tall and dark . . . Fierce as a lion. A striking young man, but always frowning. Always sad. He was sad and angry. Angry at people . . . at white people he thought were making fun of him. He was tall and dark and sad. It wasn't easy for him to be what he was. He was convinced that people were cruel and intolerant. He didn't trust anybody. He watched their every move. Their every word. Looking for hidden offense. He didn't like being what he was. His father was a black man

113

. . . in the war . . . in Germany . . . a soldier in the war. His father was a black soldier who married a German woman. After the war. During the Occupation. And Eric didn't like being what he was. He hated his mother. And he hated his father. For making him what he was. And so he was always angry. And very sad. Eric Jones was angry and sad at the world. He didn't know why. He just couldn't trust anyone. Sometimes he even accused me of saying the wrong things. But then he would realize how crazy it was, and he would get over it. He would go back to his writing, and I would go back to my painting. And we were happy for a little while. . . ."

"Enough!" Delito shouted in the utter silence of the chamber. "Laughable! This is laughable!"

But no one laughed. And no one spoke. The people on both the right and the left remained still as they gazed intently at Sitko Ghost Horse, wondering if it was possible that a demon could be so convincingly human, if it was possible for a demon to speak and feel and weep so much like a human being. They stood silently and looked from one to another, wondering if a monster could stir pity in them.

"Enough!" Delito repeated impatiently, fearful of the silence of the crowd. "I said enough!" he shouted, turning his back on Sitko and ordering the Two Horn Priests: "Take him away! He lies. Believe me when I tell you that he is cunning and that he is lying! That is what he does best! That is what he has always done! Time and again! So you must not trust him! Not for a moment! Do not be taken in by him! His story is false. His tears are false. Because he is false. He is not Sitko Ghost Horse because there is no such person. It is a trick! And fools among you have fallen for the trick! Take him away before he deceives us any more! He is not worthy of us. He

tures. She had watched over each moment of their creation. She had touched the images and she had even talked to them. And perhaps she had come to understand the magic of art.

"It doesn't matter," he lied, trying to cheer her. "I will make new pictures. All I need is paper."

"Here . . ." Patu exclaimed with relief, as she snatched up a cardboard box and gave it to Sitko. "They did not take this one. They did not take your colors. At least they did not take everything."

"No," he murmured as he gazed at her with affection. "That's what they would like to do. But they can't do it. They can never take *everything*. If I'm certain of nothing else, I'm certain of that. Perhaps they know it too, and that's what enrages them. They know that no matter what they say or what they do to me, they cannot destroy all of my pictures. They cannot erase them from the memories of people who have seen them. Maybe that's what makes them so angry and cruel. Even if they destroy my work . . . even if they destroy me . . . still they know they can never destroy what people have felt about my pictures. That part of me survives. There is very little in this world that survives, but *that* part of us survives."

Patu wiped the tears from her eyes and consoled herself by watching Sitko's rapidly moving fingers, conjuring shapes and colors, as a new image of Eric's face gradually appeared on the blank scrap of cardboard. Patu smiled broadly as the person named Eric was reborn, like a new spring out of an old winter. And when the picture was finished, Sitko placed it in her hands.

She tried to speak, but she could not do so. Her face filled with both remorse and gladness as she gently drew the scrap of cardboard to her chest and caressed it as she glanced away in embarrassment. After a long silence, she whispered: "It is good. I tell you this, it is good . . . this thing that you do with your hands. It is good, Sitko Ghost Horse."

Sitko touched her shoulder and smiled. It was the first time in many weeks that anyone had called him by his name. Her words brought tears of gratitude to his eyes, for he realized that even in this terrible and remote place where he was a stranger and a prisoner, it was possible for Patu to believe in him. And at the same time he knew that Patu understood that he also believed in her.

Neither Sitko nor Patu spoke. They simply stood in silence, nodding at one another with an expression of profound recognition—two distinctive human beings reaching across the boundless distance that separated them.

Then they quietly sat on the ground with the food bowl between them, and they had their meal together, eating frybread and dipping their fingers into a special, spicy gruel that Patu had prepared.

"In the place where you come from . . ." she asked when the meal was finished, "what do they call people who make pictures?"

"Painters . . . they call us painters."

"Yes, I remember . . . that is what you told us. Painters . . ." she repeated with confusion. "And do women also make pictures?"

"Yes, many painters are women."

"And people like me? In your world, are there men like me? Are there men who are powerful women?"

"Yes, there are people like you."

At this Patu smiled with satisfaction. "And what are they

called in your world . . . these people like me?"

Sitko did not know quite how to respond. After a moment he said: "There should be no need to give them a name."

Patu frowned. She did not seem to understand.

"Let me try to explain," Sitko said. "In my world we like to think that things stand firm. That things are one way or the other. That everything and everybody is either this or that. With nothing in between. But that's not the way it really is. I think the world is like a rainbow . . . with so many colors and so many possibilities."

Patu laughed with delight as she spread her hands in the air, making a rainbow.

"The same thing that delights you so much," Sitko said, "is very uncomfortable for most of my own people. So they don't talk about it. But people like me . . . people who are artists have always known that things are far more complicated than we like to admit. In my world there was an artist who made very strong pictures. Some people thought the pictures were ugly, but I was always fascinated by them. And I was fascinated by the artist's ideas. She said something that meant so much to me that I still remember it. She was trying to explain something about the unusual people in her pictures. And so she said that they were singular people who appeared to her from somewhere farther out than we are. Beckoned but not driven. People invented by belief. She said that the people in her pictures were both the creators and the heroes of a real dream . . . a dream by which our own courage and cunning are tested and tried; so that we may wonder all over again what is veritable and inevitable and possible and what it is to become whoever we may be."

Patu frowned and shook her head in confusion.

"It is not important," Sitko said quietly. "In my world we need to talk about things that baffle us. We are still trying to figure out who we are. But for you, Patu, it seems to be quite different."

Patu laughed. "Sometimes you say very funny things, Sitko Ghost Horse!" she exclaimed with a husky giggle. "Sometimes I think maybe you have a big wind in your head."

"Sometimes I think you may be right," Sitko answered, and smiled broadly.

"But now, Sitko Ghost Horse, you must tell me the truth. You must tell me about *out there*," she whispered with a glint of fear in her eyes. "I want to know about this other place where you come from. And I want to know about your people. Tell me about this man named Eric Jones. Tell me about the people who make pictures. When you were out there, what did you do with the pictures you made, Sitko Ghost Horse? Tell me all of these things so I can understand."

"It is very complicated, what you ask, Patu," Sitko said with uncertainty. "Let me see. How can I explain?" he said with a sigh of amusement and exasperation. "I guess it all starts in my studio . . . which is the name of the place where I work. You see, for a long time Eric and I had a studio in the city. It was a very big, empty space. It had very high ceilings," Sitko said, using gestures to outline the studio in the air. "A tall roof . . . very high . . . that's right . . . and walls made of red bricks like the walls of your village . . . only red instead of gray. That's right," he laughed as Patu began to imitate the movements of his hands, making her own studio in the air. "And over here . . . in this corner is where Eric worked. Yes, right there. Can you see it? The walls in his corner were covered with books. All the way to the roof. Hundreds and hundreds of books. I used to be frightened to death every time a truck passed for fear he would be buried alive in an avalanche of falling books!" Sitko exclaimed with a smile. Then his expression darkened as he thought about Eric Jones. "So many books . . . so many books," he said sadly, letting his hands fall to his sides.

"And tell me, Sitko Ghost Horse," Patu asked, "where did you make your pictures in this studio?"

"Here . . ." he answered, coming out of his depressed mood and smiling at Patu. "In this corner . . . all the way at the other end of the studio. That was my place. And God help anybody who tried to clean it up! The walls were splattered with paint. Colors everywhere! All the colors I used to make my pictures. Piles of twisted and crumpled tubes of paint. Piles and piles of them. And lots of peanut butter bottles filled with paintbrushes. And a big sheet of window glass on which I mixed my colors. Ultramarine Blue and Titanium White. What marvelous names! Burnt Sienna and Viridian. Yellow Ocher and Cadmium Yellow. A whole mountain of colors. And there was always the smell of the paints and the solvents. It was wonderful! Like nothing else in the world. And there was always music. And there were friends all hours of the night. Richard and Carlos. Averna and Lucia. Susan and Leonard. So many friends. We sprawled on the floor and ate pizza and drank red wine. And of course we talked and talked. Lord, how we talked! Eric and I really loved that studio. It took us years to get it. Because in my world, you have to sell your pictures and you have to publish your stories if you want to have a place like our studio. You have to sell a lot of things, otherwise you are too poor to have the kind of life Eric and I had."

"So your people paid you to put their faces on paper?"

"Yes . . ." Sitko said with an amused smile. "Sometimes they paid me. But I didn't make pictures just of people. I made pictures of just about everything and sometimes I made pictures about nothing!"

Sitko fell silent, gazing past Patu as a breeze flew into the room. Crickets sang and somewhere there was the rumble of a subway train. Sitko was standing in front of his easel, studying the image that appeared as his brush moved across the canvas. His eyes traveled slowly back and forth from his painting to his model. As the paintbrush moved, he could feel a succession of impulses moving from his eyes into his hands. His fingers had a life of their own. And gradually a figure began to appear on the canvas. It was a male nude, bold, sensual, and mysterious.

Eric grumbled with discomfort as he sat on a stool, growing increasingly impatient as Sitko formed his body.

"Don't move . . . please. It is only going to take a few more minutes," Sitko urged, gazing at Eric and rapidly transforming his body into a succession of colors and lines.

Then a truck backfired and suddenly the breeze vanished from the room.

"Everything and nothing?" Patu was saying.

"Yes, everything and nothing," he answered, looking down at his hands. "Sometimes I painted Eric and sometimes I painted nothing in particular . . . just some forms that flashed through my mind. And while I painted, Eric sat at his desk and wrote. For nine years I painted and he wrote. We both worked hard. All the time. Day and night. Because it takes years before anybody notices your work. Then, one day, everything changed for us."

"What happened on the day that everything changed?" Patu asked expectantly.

Sitko laughed with an ironic expression on his face. "What happened? I'll tell you what happened. A nobody who thought he was somebody told everybody else that I was no longer a nobody. Just like that! Somehow or other I became a *somebody*! And, remarkably enough, everybody believed it! Ha!"

"Ha!" Patu echoed, without seeming to understand the word. "HA!"

"So things began to change for Eric and me. And that was very good and it was also not very good."

"Good and not good?" Patu questioned.

"That's right. You see, we finally had all the things we wanted. We even took a trip. On an airplane . . . way up in the sky and across the ocean."

"Up in the sky?"

"And for a while it was marvelous! Eric was so proud of me! He loved to go to all the parties at galleries . . . when my pictures were put on the walls so people could look at them," Sitko said, overcome by memories.

"Like these walls?" asked Patu. "Like the pictures that you made here?"

"Yes, like these walls . . . just like these walls," Sitko murmured, sadly recalling the lost days.

An enormous room filled with light. And in the light many

floating images. Time adrift, filling the space with distant voices and faces. In a very large and very white space. Friends and music and laughter.

"There were lots of peculiar people and critics and friends. They came to the gallery for reasons of their own. And they looked at my pictures and talked and talked," Sitko said with a nostalgic smile.

"Critics . . . and friends?" Patu repeated with confusion.

"Yes, friends and strangers and critics," Sitko said. Then he grinned at Patu and explained, "You know what friends and strangers are. And I won't even *try* to tell you what critics are!"

Sitko laughed and Patu joined in his laughter, although she had no idea why he was laughing.

Bright light in an enormous room. Unbridled time floating recklessly in the light.

Those were good days for Sitko. But Eric's writing was not well received. He sat motionless for hours staring at his typewriter. But the words he wanted eluded him. Sitko admired Eric's talent, but people were not interested in what Eric wrote. And this created tension between Sitko and Eric.

"How can I write if I don't believe a word I say?" Eric exclaimed. "It's easy for you. You just throw paint on a canvas!"

"Come on, Eric . . ."

"Don't placate me, goddammit! Don't start placating me with all that flattery and bullshit! You've got talent and I don't! That's what it comes down to, doesn't it? That's what everybody thinks and that's what you think!"

Sitko sighed and shrugged in resignation. "What can I say?"

"Please don't say anything! And don't be so damn understanding all the time!"

"Okay, I won't be understanding. I'll be an asshole like you! What would you like me to say? Should I just tell you to go to hell?"

"Sure! Why not? What do you need with me? Everybody is always gazing at you like you're some kind of Adonis! There's a fucking line of people two miles long, just waiting for me to clear out of your life! So what the hell do you need with a flunky like me? You make all the money. You get paid for everything you paint. Like clockwork! And me . . . I've yet to sell a word I've written. I just live here! I'm the goddam family dog! I don't mean shit around here. You paid for the studio. Everything in here belongs to you! You even pay for my fucking typing paper! And what the hell do I contribute?"

"It doesn't bother me, Eric," Sitko said with a weary gesture. "So why does it bother you?"

"It bothers me a lot!" Eric shouted. "A whole lot! And things are getting worse. Wherever we go, people talk to you but they just ignore me. They look at you like you're something to eat. Do you have any idea how damn beautiful you are? And do you know how fucking mad it gets me when I look at you?"

"Come on, Eric, you don't mean that. . . ."

"Okay . . . okay . . . so I don't mean it. But you've got to understand how rough it is on me. I already feel so unimportant. So why the hell am I living with someone that everybody thinks is a living god?"

Sitko affectionately grasped Eric by the shoulders. "For years and years nobody gave a damn about me," Sitko said, as he sat next to Eric. "You were the only one who cared

125

what happened to me. Do you think I've forgotten that?"

"Bullshit . . ." Eric muttered. "You're too good for me. What the hell do you want with somebody like me? That's what I always try to figure out. You can't be for real if you give a shit about somebody like me."

"That's crazy," Sitko exclaimed. "You dumb fruit! What the hell are you talking about?"

The two men looked at one another, and suddenly they began to laugh.

"That's better," Sitko said with a broad smile. "Isn't it crazy . . . everything was just fine between you and me when neither of us had a dime. Then, all of a sudden, people I never gave a damn about wanted to talk to me. But the only reason they bother is because somebody told them I'm supposed to be hot shit. Otherwise they couldn't be bothered. And so I get a lot of attention. And I don't blame you if it pisses you off. But some of my friends are okay. They understand what I'm painting. And I can't help it if that makes me feel terrific. But a lot them know nothing about my work and couldn't care less. They just hang around and gaze at me like I'm going to sprout wings. But I'm not an idiot, Eric. I realize that most of them just want to get into my pants."

"And that's supposed to make me happy?" Eric muttered as he got up and paced slowly back and forth in the enormous room filled with light. Sitko watched his friend, drifting farther and farther away from him. Time pulled free of the walls and filled the vast, white space with distant voices and faces.

For a moment everything stopped.

Then Patu made a sound full of melancholy.

"So anyway," Sitko said, "I got a lot of attention. And I won't deny it, I enjoyed every minute of it. But at the same time, I could see that Eric's pride in me was changing into something else. He started to get sullen and bitter. He no longer looked at me with admiration, but with anger and envy. He found fault with everything I did. It angered me. It made me sad. But I didn't know what to do. Gradually, Eric retreated. Vanishing from my life. Disappearing into the crowd. I remember him at parties, standing alone against a wall. Not talking. To anybody."

Again everything stopped.

Then there was a barrage of voices and laughter and music. A circle of young men and elderly women gazed with fascination at Sitko as he tried to answer their questions. He was delighted by the attention but he could not concentrate on what he was saying. Instead he watched Eric, standing by himself, with a drink in his hand. Everyone seemed to ignore him. At first he made efforts to talk to people, but he could not seem to connect, and he sank into his isolation. Soon he began drinking heavily.

The room filled with people—writers and painters and musicians; people whom Sitko wanted Eric to get to know. But every time he tried to approach Eric, someone would pull him away to introduce him to arriving guests. "I'll be right back," Sitko whispered. "I'm sorry . . ."

When Sitko finally returned to Eric, he introduced him to some of the people whose work he admired. But they said only a few words to Eric, and then they turned their backs on him and walked away.

"I'm sorry . . ." Sitko murmured as he looked into Eric's angry eyes. "I know it's terrible, but what can I do?"

"I'll tell you what you can do! You can tear yourself away from your fans and get your goddam coat so we can get the hell out of here! That's what you can do!"

Bursting into the frigid night air, Eric was bristling with rage, as if somebody had insulted him to his face. "Fucking assholes, that's what they are! A bunch of self-important, do-nothing assholes!"

"That's not true, Eric, and you know it. There were some remarkable people there."

"Well, screw all your remarkable people! As far as I'm concerned they're just a bunch of racist assholes! Can you fucking believe the way they turned their backs on me! Can you believe it!"

Sitko started to object but shook his head in frustration and fell silent as the two friends walked down the icy street.

Footsteps echoed in the silence, until Patu sighed and gazed down at the drawing of Eric, as if she were trying to see him more clearly.

"So," Sitko said with a shrug, "it was a good time and it was also a bad time. I had finally made a name for myself. But there were still lots of problems. For one thing, the name I had made for myself wasn't my own name. It was the name I had been given by my foster father. And I always hated it. So I did something crazy. After years of trying to get people to know who I was, I announced that I was somebody else! I stopped being Seymour Miller and changed back into Sitko Ghost Horse! God knows what most people must have thought! In my world you just don't do things like that. But I did it anyway, and somehow I survived. But only for a while. I soon learned something terrible about people."

Patu nodded with concern. "Is that when you came into the desert?" she asked. "Is that when you left your people and came to our village?"

"No . . ." Sitko murmured. "That was later. After the sickness came."

"Ah . . ." Patu whispered, "the sickness." Then she fell silent.

In the dark silence that overtook them, Sitko gazed sadly at the blank walls of the little prison where he had drawn images of his friends. Now they were gone. All the people of his life had been buried alive under a coat of whitewash. They had been wiped away, erased from the world. And yet, even now, when Sitko listened carefully, he was certain that somewhere beneath the whitewash his friends and their voices continued to live. They cried out to be remembered. When he pressed his hands to the walls he could hear them imploring to be set free. And hearing their voices, he realized something astounding. The cry for help did not come from the walls. It was coming from within his own body. And suddenly Sitko realized that the most precious people of his life were still alive and living somewhere within his hands and fingertips.

"I have spent a great deal of my life trying to make pictures of the things I love. I wonder if that isn't a terrible waste of time. I've tried to understand my motives, but I can't understand why I do it. I just have to make pictures! It's like an obsession. I sometimes feel that painting is all that stands between me and death. So my pictures are like a haunting . . . perched on the brink . . . created at that dark and dangerous place where images border on extinction. So I have no choice. I must keep the people and things I love alive in my pictures. And yet, despite all the feeling I put into my paintings, there are always people who are enraged by them. I don't understand it. Some people act as if I am deliberately trying to offend them. But that's not what I'm doing. I make pictures because I must. I don't think I would do it otherwise, because making art is the most naked and vulnerable thing a person can do. Opening yourself to the scrutiny of strangers. Hoping they will be touched by what you have made. Hoping they will cherish the fragile things you have put down on paper or canvas. And when they don't understand and when they get angry, it makes a mess of my whole life. And to tell you the truth, it's very nearly as bad when people like what I paint for the wrong reasons. Either way it doesn't make sense. They hate my guts or they adore me. That's the way it's always been. In the orphanage. In school. In the house of Alexander Milas-Miller. And then it started to happen at the galleries where I showed my pictures.''

"What happened to you, Sitko Ghost Horse?" Patu urged.

Sitko did not answer. He looked out the window, into a light that blinded him.

"What happened to you in the world out there?" Patu asked again as she approached Sitko and gently shook him. But Sitko did not respond. He stood silently, gazing aimlessly into a light coming from another time and another place.

Sitko was nervous. He kept fidgeting with the buttons of his shirt until Eric gave him an exasperated look.

"For godsake, will you stop! You're making me crazy! How many times do I have to tell you that everything is going to be fine?"

Despite Eric's reassurance, Sitko was anxious. He had worked for more than a year on the new paintings, but he was uncertain how people would react to them.

The subject matter was completely new for him. He had never painted with such directness and sexual candor. Even the style was a drastic departure from the kind of folk imagery that had earned him a reputation.

"Why shouldn't I worry?" Sitko exclaimed. "There's plenty to worry about. People don't like you to change. In fact, they hate it. Everybody was very happy with the old stuff I did. All that *Home on the Range* stuff was what they expected from me. They liked to think of me as an exotic creature. So who knows how they'll react to the new paintings? You saw the disgusted look on Frank Adams's face when he saw my new work! Chrisake, he looked embarrassed, like he had walked in on somebody having sex! So tell me, what was all of that supposed to mean?"

"Who knows what it meant? If he's not bitching about somebody, he isn't happy!" Eric exclaimed, pulling Sitko's hands away from the buttons. "Frank Adams is an opinionated asshole. You know that and I know that! Every time we see him he goes on and on about his ethnic pride and all the other bullshit he's made into a career for himself!"

"Come on, Eric, he's a friend."

"A friend, my ass. A friend doesn't chip away at you day in and day out. He won't say it straight out, but he's forever implying something unpleasant about how we live and what we do. He might as well come right out and say it. He thinks we're a couple of pussies because we prefer to do our work instead of marching in the street and fighting the good fight. Every time he comes over here he stands around in all his Afro drag counting how many *people of color* we did or didn't invite. It makes me sick. Because he really couldn't give a shit.

He loves to talk on and on about art that deals with social issues, but in his little lily-white heart he thinks everybody should still be painting French landscapes! So why let him bother you?"

Sitko shrugged and began to play with the buttons of his shirt. Now he was even more nervous. And Eric wasn't helping his frame of mind. He had been drinking all afternoon and was getting more and more surly as the hour for the opening drew near.

"Why don't you let up on the booze?" Sitko murmured when Eric refilled his glass.

"Why don't you stop worrying about what I do?" Eric shot back with a dark look.

"If you want to make things worse, just keep on drinking! That's all I need tonight!"

"I'll do whatever I want to do!" Eric barked, his words getting thick and slurred. "How the hell do you expect me to face that bunch of assholes you call your friends? Believe me, I need to be half blind to deal with all their superior bullshit!"

Suzanne, the gallery owner, grumbled with annoyance as she trailed through the blinding white space, placing a huge floral arrangement on the table at the entrance. "How about giving it a rest?" she growled at Eric and Sitko. "Or have you forgotten? This is supposed to be fun. So lighten up, for godsake. And Eric, you can do me a major favor tonight. Just push a dozen canapés in your big mouth and shut up!"

Eric ignored her remark and lifted his drink to his lips, finishing it in one long gulp. Then he banged down the glass and stared defiantly at Sitko and Suzanne as he refilled it to the brim. Sitko shook his head in disgust and followed Suzanne into the adjoining galleries, where his pictures glowed in the bright light.

He slowly surveyed the paintings, trying to get some hint of what others might see, but every mass of color, every texture and line was so familiar that he could not imagine how others would see his work. The light flickered. And his paintings would not rest. They moved across his memory. Flashes of light. A long dream of faces. Images from every day of his life. There was nothing here that he had not seen before in some remote place behind his eyes. The paintings were his life. His entire life falling through space, collapsing inward upon itself endlessly. Everything he had ever seen or painted was awash in the white light. Fleeting. A thousand people traced upon the walls. Colors. Burning bright. Fire and blood. Evoking ghosts and monsters. Calling out their names. Begging to be heard. Until a drumming filled the room. And Grandma Amana appeared in a corner, endlessly rocking as her eyes filled with bright blue light. "Listen, child," she whispered as the walls devoured her image, "you must learn to look at the world twice. First you must bring your eyes together in front so you can see each droplet of rain on the grass, so you can see the smoke rising from an anthill in the sunshine. Nothing should escape your notice. Now you must learn to look again, with your eyes at the very edge of what is visible. Now you must see dimly if you wish to see things that are dim—the dark place where the animal tracks are still fresh. You must learn to look at the world twice if you wish to see all that there is to see."

Sitko gasped and swung around, only to discover that it was Suzanne who had touched his sleeve.

"Are you all right?" she asked in a strange voice.

"Yes . . ." he murmured, as he watched his grandmother vanish into the colors, burning bright, fire and blood. "Yes, I'm fine," he whispered, as he watched Reno out of the corner of his eye, fleeing into the darkness of an open door and leaving only a twisted shadow upon the gallery wall.

"God," Sitko moaned, "what am I doing here? They'll destroy me. I've known it all along . . . they want to destroy me."

"You really are worried," Suzanne said, coming to his side and putting her arm around his shoulder. "Look, guy, you're good. Just remember that. I've seen a lot of crap in my time. But you're good."

"Thanks," Sitko murmured. "I don't mean to be a baby. But when the paintings are finally hung on the walls, all of a sudden I begin to see them differently. And it scares the hell out of me! I guess I never think about the fact that all kinds of people will be looking at this stuff when I'm painting. But now, as I look at all of these canvases, one after another, all over the place, I get a little worried."

"Don't worry. Just enjoy yourself."

"Okay. But tell me the truth, Suzanne. Do you think there's going to be any problem about the nudes?"

"Come on!" Suzanne laughed with astonishment. "You gotta be kidding! What's the problem here? A few private parts? A little sex? Some dicks, some assholes? A bunch of guys doing it? You don't really think that anybody around here is going to give a shit! I wish they would! I'd love it! What we need is a real sensation. But, my dear boy, there's nothing you or anybody else could do that's outrageous. We're far beyond that point. It's as simple as that. So go have a drink before Eric finishes every bottle in the place, and settle

134

down and enjoy all the fuss and flattery! This is your night to have some fun and it's my night to make some money!"

Sitko felt a bit better. He kissed Suzanne on the cheek and wandered off, meandering peacefully through the gallery, looking at the images with new eyes and feeling a rising excitement in the knowledge that soon every inch of the place would be filled with noisy and opinionated people. Whatever they might think of his new work, they were still the only people who cared about painting. They were island people, living in floating communities beyond the city limits—separate, alien, and powered by an obsession to create something. Crazy people, but they were his people. The people of his strange little ghetto, driven underground by equal measures of indifference and animosity. They were outcasts who had gathered into little protective groups, in a ramshackle district where rents were low and neighborhood morality was easygoing. No one was ever alarmed if a painter's lights were on till five in the morning or if a musician's stereo jarred the dawn. The old-timers who sat out among the garbage cans on hot summer evenings were unimpressed by the young people who endlessly hauled trash out of their tiny flats, where they were transforming squalor into slum-elegance. The old people who had stayed on were not easily fazed by anything. They shrugged indifferently as they watched the island people descend upon their fading neighborhood. They rejected nothing. They resented nothing. Not the fantastic young bearded window gardener tending his marijuana crop at midnight and not the odd assorted couples of mixed colors and shapes.

Beyond the wide, scrubbed windows of Suzanne's gallery the world was dank and soiled. In the street, the pavement was cracked and gutted. Manhole covers were missing, leaving gaping holes from which clouds of thick gray steam billowed. Water trickled incessantly from rusty fire hydrants. And under coats of thick paint loomed the buried beauty of old cast-iron buildings. Now and again, from underground, came the distant, mysterious rumble of trains darting like rats beneath the city. In the late afternoon, Sitko could hear the churning of machinery echoing among the air shafts. Billows of soot flew out of open windows and chimneys. Trucks rumbled to and fro in the trash-filled streets, where mangy cats crept along filthy gutters and disappeared into storm drains.

Thousands of working people had poured into the streets, jubilant to be liberated from the sweatshops perched in airless lofts where they worked all day, making ugly, frilly dresses for children. Their voices had rung out in the elevator shafts, rocketing upward and intruding upon the uppermost floors where artists were still asleep. Now as the evening came down upon the streets and pale streetlights blinked on, workingmen clutched their groins as they glared at the women. They shouted lurid remarks and they urinated against the buildings. The women gossiped and laughed as they made purchases at makeshift shops operated out of the backs of trucks, carrying away huge fishes wrapped carelessly in newspaper. Then the workers made a great racket as they rushed into the bowels of the city, where they crowded into monstrously defiled trains that took them away to distant ghettos of their own.

Now it was dark, and the small crowd of artists across the street was slowly disbanding, deserting poet Ralston Farina and his friends, who had made a "time piece" in chalk on the sidewalk. The lights in the factories had gone out, and the managers in their suits and ties trampled over Ralston's frail handiwork as they hustled between the unhurried artists.

Now it was night. Yellow light filled the air. The transient people had gone home. And the ghetto belonged to those who had been left behind. Along the back streets, above the decrepit and barred factories, above the new boutiques and cafés, countless windows were filled with light and plants and the outline of island people engaged in their own time and space.

It was a few days after the exhibition that Suzanne called and told Sitko that she had gotten a letter.

"It's got to be a joke," she said.

"Who is it from?" Sitko asked. "And who would joke about something like that?"

"All I know is that they say they don't want to be associated with the kind of paintings I've been showing. Can you believe it?"

"But why would they do something like that?"

"I have no idea," Suzanne said. "But I'm going to fight it. After all . . . since when can they tell people what they can and can't exhibit? Don't worry about it. I said I'd show your work and nobody is going to stop me from doing it. We'll talk soon, but I've got to go. Call me."

"Christ!" Sitko groaned when Suzanne hung up.

"What's going on?" Eric shouted from his desk.

Sitko walked aimlessly from one end of the studio to the other and stood glumly beneath Eric's towering shelves of books.

When Eric saw the expression on Sitko's face he hurried

to his side. "What's the matter? You look terrible."

"There's a lot of trouble about my paintings," Sitko said. "They say they're offensive."

"What do you mean, *offensive*?"

"They say they're pornographic. That they're disgusting. Can you believe it?"

"What are you talking about . . . *pornographic*?"

"I don't know. All I know is that Suzanne got a letter. She sounded okay, but I have no idea what's going to happen now."

"It's got to be some kind of mistake. Listen to me, Sitko, don't get worked up about it. The show was a tremendous success. Everybody loved it. Jesus, even Frank Adams said nice things about it. Everybody was delighted that you were doing something new. So let Suzanne handle it. It's bound to be okay. After all, they can't just piss on you like that! You've got a tremendous reputation!"

Sitko shook his head in confusion as a terrible exhaustion overtook him.

"Look, Sitko," Eric murmured as he took his friend by the shoulders and smiled at him with reassurance. "It's going to be fine. You'll see. It's just like the old story my dad used to tell me when people were nasty to me. He told about a bunch of ratty old chickens that were so skinny and so mangy that they didn't have any feathers and couldn't even fly. All they could do was cackle and cackle and run around the barnyard, quarreling with one another. Well, one day they looked way up in the sky, and lo and behold there was some kind of bird flying around high as the clouds. Well, those nasty old chickens started to cackle louder than ever, pointing up into the sky and shouting insults at that beautiful eagle that was soaring high above them . . . higher than they could ever dream of going."

Sitko smiled reluctantly and embraced Eric.

"So don't you worry," Eric said with a bright smile. "Like my daddy always used to say, 'Don't you be bothered about them mangy old chickens when they shout insults at you.' They're just a bunch of chickens. And they're mad because they can never in a million years soar high up in the sky. And they can never see all the wonderful things that you can see from way up in your special place high in the sky."

Three days later, Suzanne called again.

"You had better get down here right away," she said in a sullen tone. "We've got trouble. I just got a phone call from some crazy guy who claims you're a fake."

"A fake!" Sitko exclaimed. "Who said I'm a fake?"

Eric grabbed the phone out of Sitko's hand and shouted: "What does that mean? What the hell kind of craziness is this?"

"Look, I don't know what's going on. First I got a letter and now I've gotten a phone call from some loony claiming he's got a shoebox full of proof that Sitko isn't who he says he is. Somebody's out to make trouble. And I don't have the slightest idea what's going on, but you and Sitko had better come down here right away so we can talk before this thing gets out of hand."

Eric and Sitko were about to rush out the door when the telephone rang again.

"No, you can't speak to him!" Eric shouted into the phone. "Who are you supposed to be? Well, what do you want?"

"What's going on?" Sitko exclaimed nervously, when he saw the expression of panic that filled Eric's face.

"No, I already said you can't talk to him!" Eric shouted into the phone. "You can't be serious. This whole thing is a lot of crap." And with that he slammed down the receiver.

"I don't think you should have done that," Sitko mumbled as a wave of dread overtook him.

"Why the hell not?" Eric shouted. "This asshole reporter wanted to know if your real name is Seymour Miller! Can you believe such crap? He said that some guy says that there's no such person as Sitko Ghost Horse! What was I supposed to say to him? What can you say to somebody who's crazy enough to believe such shit?"

"Maybe I should call back and at least try to talk sense with him," Sitko said with urgency, sensing that something dreadful was coming down on him.

"He doesn't want to hear you talk sense," Eric exclaimed in a rage. "Come on, Sitko, try to see what's going on here," he urged as he took Sitko's hand to comfort him. "Can't you see what's happening here? Somebody's got some kind of gripe against you. And you're being lynched. That's what's happening. You're being lynched! That smart-aleck reporter wants to wipe the floor with your ass! And goddammit, we're not going to let him get away with it!"

By the time Sitko and Eric arrived at the gallery, the reporter was on the telephone with Suzanne.

"I can't believe this is happening. It's a madhouse around

here," Suzanne exclaimed. "I really don't think I can handle all of this! I've never heard such crazies!"

Sitko glared out the windows into the yellow smoke that billowed from the gutters. A tide of newspaper and trash suddenly flew into the air and hovered above the dark buildings. There was the sound of a siren. And then the wind stopped and a storm of feathers silently floated into the street, piling up against the windows. He gasped as he saw a group of men slowly approaching the gallery, swinging their arms and shouting.

"Who are those people?" Sitko whispered in dread, pointing at the men as they pressed their massive faces against the windows.

"What are you talking about? What are you trying to say?" Suzanne exclaimed as she shook her head in bewilderment and said, "I really don't know what's going on. All I know is that I'm totally exhausted from all of this. Maybe you can explain. I think the least you owe me is an explanation."

"An explanation for what?" Eric shouted.

"All I know is that we've got a bunch of fanatics claiming that Sitko's paintings glorify perversion."

"What do they mean—*perversion*?" Eric bellowed as Sitko stared in dread at the men who ran their tongues against the windows of the gallery, leaving jagged snail trails on the glass.

"Calm down and try to listen to what I'm telling you," Suzanne urged. "They're threatening to burn down my gallery, for godsake. Do you hear what I'm saying? They're crazy. And they say they'll burn me out if I don't pull Sitko's show."

Sitko shuddered as newspaper and trash billowed from the

gutters. There was a siren and the faint sound of children weeping. Somewhere beyond the windows of the gallery. In the world.

"Sitko—are you listening to me?" Suzanne exclaimed. "Some reporter is telling me that you're not who you say you are. He says that you're really a Jew named Seymour Miller."

"My name is Sitko Ghost Horse," Sitko muttered without taking his eyes from the window. "My name is Sitko Ghost Horse."

"They're saying that your name is really Seymour Miller and that you've been appropriating somebody else's culture and degrading it with your art. That's what they're saying."

"Incredible," Sitko mumbled, as a storm of dead birds fell into the street, piling up against the windows and covering the bodies of the men who pressed their groins to the glass.

"What are you saying?" Suzanne shouted. "Answer me!"

Sitko covered his face and slumped into a chair.

"I need to know what this is all about," Suzanne pleaded, an expression coming over her face that was entirely unfamiliar to Sitko.

"Look, Suzanne," Eric shouted into her face, "don't give us that bullshit! You are supposed to show some loyalty here. You know what I mean? You know damn well that Sitko used to be called Seymour Miller. You know he was adopted. So don't all of a sudden act so fucking surprised!"

"Look, guys," she muttered with undisguised disdain, "I'm just trying to sell paintings. You know what I mean? I can't get involved in all this crap. So you'll just have to excuse me, 'cause I'm going home! *You* can talk to those maniacs and sort it out."

"Wait just one fucking minute," Eric shouted.

"I'm not waiting for anybody or for anything! I'm going home."

"Great! That's just fucking great!" Eric exclaimed, striding over to Sitko and looking down on him. "She turned out to be some friend, right! Some fucking friend!"

"Let's go," Sitko muttered. "Let her go home and let's just get out of here."

"I'm sorry . . ." Suzanne said softly as she put her arm around Sitko. "I'm just not the political type, and all of this stuff scares the shit out of me."

"Great! All of the sudden she's a pussy cat! Just fucking great!"

Suzanne glared at Eric. "Why don't you cool out, asshole. What do you know about me anyway!"

Then she kissed Sitko. "I'm really sorry," she whispered, as she left them on the pavement in front of the gallery.

Sitko's head reeled. He opened his mouth in despair and turned around, trying to silence the voices that echoed in his ears. Suddenly the wind burst against the walls of the gallery, sending up a blinding tide of yellow smoke. Sitko struggled forward against the gust, staring with amazement at the huge figures relentlessly marching toward them, cursing and shouting and laughing as their eyes glowed in the smoke.

"What have I done?" Sitko cried out. "Why are you doing this to me?"

A great hulk of a person slowly turned upon Sitko and Eric, rumbling as he moved. "Who are you?" a terrible voice demanded. "You!" the man shouted as he pointed at Sitko. "Who are you?"

"My name is Sitko Ghost Horse."

"What does that mean?" the man demanded, as he glared at Sitko and stepped forward into the light. A trail of sweat flowed from beneath the man's helmet and covered his featureless face. "Where do you come from? Who are your people?"

"My name is Sitko Ghost Horse!" Sitko repeated in a shout. "My name is Sitko Ghost Horse! But I don't know where I come from. My grandmother was called Amana! Her husband was Far Away Son! But he died. She had a child. With a stranger. That child was my mother, Jemina Bonneville! And my father was called Jamie Ghost Horse! And my foster father was named Alexander Milas-Miller. And when I was adopted I was called Seymour Miller. They called me Sy Miller, but I am Sitko Ghost Horse. That is who I am!"

The man leered as he said to the others: "This asshole doesn't know that his real name is *pussy*!"

Eric pulled Sitko out of the man's reach and shouted, "Back off, and get the fuck out of my face!"

"Look, nigger," the man yelled, as the crowd advanced upon them, "we don't want to mess with you. It's your faggot friend we're after!"

"Just ignore them," Sitko urged. "Forget about it, Eric, and let's get the hell out of here."

But Eric could not endure the baiting and insults. When one of the protesters spit in his face and called him a queer, Eric took a swing at him, sending him flying. There was a great shout of anger from the protesters as the man crashed to the pavement. And then a hail of leaflets came raining down on Sitko and Eric.

"Let's get out of here!" Sitko pleaded. But Eric stood his ground, glaring at their tormentors, possessed by a surge of bitterness and pain. Suddenly he grabbed one of the men and began to shake him until his shirt ripped from his body and he crashed against the windows of the gallery.

"I don't take that kind of shit from anybody!" Eric was shouting again and again as he shook the man. "Do you hear what I'm saying, you dumb sonofabitch? I won't take that shit from you or anybody else!" he shouted as he darted after another man, grabbed him, and began to smash his head against the window.

"Stop it, Eric!" Sitko shouted, trying to restrain his friend, whose rage had turned into such overwhelming power that Sitko could not break his grasp on the man's shoulders. "For godsake, you're going to kill him!"

Then, abruptly, Eric released the man, who fell back in a daze.

"Come on! Right now," Sitko muttered, glancing nervously at the people blocking their way. "Let's go."

The protesters slowly backed away. Eric and Sitko cautiously made their way toward the street, panting and staying close together. Just as they were clear of the men, Sitko glanced back and caught sight of someone slowly reaching toward the ground. There was something about the man's gesture that sent a chill through Sitko. Suddenly there was a blast as a rock shot through the air and shattered the window above Eric. There was a burst of glass splinters. A roar echoed among the deserted buildings. Eric cried out. He winced and tottered as he began to slide down a wall to the ground, enveloped by the steam rising from the storm drains. For a moment no one moved. Then everyone scattered. Someone shouted for the police from a window. But it was too late. Sitko knelt over Eric, clutching him as he bled.

* * *

Somewhere a clock was striking the hour. Ten thousand moths collided in the air. An owl shrieked. A large brown rat raced across the sky. And the Moon drew back her silver lips and showed her ferocious teeth.

Sitko leaned against the wall and stared down at the blood that covered him. He began to shout, until someone gently embraced him. He pulled away and groaned. "It will be all right . . ." a voice whispered. He gasped in fear and slowly turned and looked into Patu's worried face. "Sitko Ghost Horse . . ." she said, "what is happening to you?"

He gasped again as Patu's face changed, first into his mother and then into the loathsome Moon. He cringed and spun around, running down the hall, searching the empty rooms for his brother. "Reno! Reno!" Then someone touched him. He sobbed in terror and turned to stare into the eyes of a nurse. "It will be all right . . ." she said.

But it was not all right. He could not catch his breath. He could not keep his balance.

"What's the matter with you? Are you all right?" the nurse asked.

Sitko could not respond. He was balanced on the brink, tottering between memory and extinction. He could not keep his footing. His feet were far below, rooted in a painted landscape, covered with crimson. Above him was a vast explosion of yellow light. Bursting over his head again and again as the air rocked with an endless roll of thunder. In the distance, someone leaned far out a high window, calling for help. But it was too late. Sitko whirled around to face the people surrounding him. He shouted when he saw a man reaching into his pocket. Then there was a burst. Someone fell to the ground and squirmed in agony. Another burst. And another. Bodies falling to the ground. Sitko wailed as blood geysered upward and drenched his face and filled his eyes. He whimpered when he saw Eric turn crimson. Above him the sky was on fire. He shuddered as he lurched and fell into the flames. Falling. He reached out and desperately clung to his mother. But she was angry. "Stop it!" she said. "My God, child, will you stop crying!" Then she took his hand and led him away. He clung to her, but a ferocious wind blew them apart, thrusting him out into perpetual darkness. And then he began to fall again. And as he fell he looked back and saw his father walking up a driveway and reaching into his pocket. There was a furious clap of thunder and another shot rang out. A man fell to the ground screaming. Someone fell in a heap, twitching on the ground as his intestines slithered out of a great wound in his belly. Thunder rolled off the buildings. And Sitko wept helplessly and watched the tall, dark man open the door of the car where his mother sat, frozen with fear.

Now Sitko began to plummet, calling again and again for his brother. "Reno!" he shouted. "You've got to help me!"

The sound vanished as suddenly as it began. The world spun around and stopped. It was silent. There was no sound but the clatter of dishes. Now the darkness was gone, and when he opened his eyes, he was in a restaurant. Reno and his mother were seated across from him, quietly talking.

"It is such a nice home for both of you," Jemina was saying with tears in her eyes. "Such a wonderful opportunity for all of us. So you've got to go to Alexander and explain that you're sorry."

147

"It's no use," Reno said, twisting his napkin. "It's no use. . . ."

"Don't say that. Please don't say that. I want you to talk to him," she whispered, her eyes darting frantically from side to side. "You just have to come home and make it up to him!"

"It's no good, Mom," Reno said. "It'll never happen. Don't you see, it's finished."

Jemina began to cry, and Reno leaned toward Sitko and said that a buzzer was going off in his head. He said he had water dripping inside his head. He stared at their mother and whispered into Sitko's ear, saying he didn't trust the strange woman at their table.

Sitko stared at his brother, watching in dread as something terrible began to happen in Reno's face. There was a tidal wave rising in the space behind his brother's eyes, as if his brain were exploding. He didn't know what to do as his mother wept and Reno began to vanish into thin air.

"Listen, Mom, I really have to take Reno home . . ." he begged in desperation, knowing that at any moment something terrible was going to happen.

"No . . . no . . . don't do that, Sitko. Please don't leave yet. You've got to listen to what I'm telling you. It's for your own good. You never took the time to get to know Alexander. Believe me, he's a good man. He doesn't mean anybody any harm. He gave us a home and everything money could buy. He took us in when nobody would have us, Sitko. He's not a bad man, believe me. So listen to me, honey, you've got to call him, do you hear? And you've got to tell him how sorry you are," she begged in a pathetic little voice. "For my sake, Sitko, for me, you have to do this for me. You've got to make him listen so both of you can come home to me where you belong!"

Reno moaned. Sitko anxiously glanced toward his brother. He looked as if he were drowning. His head was shaking and he was gasping for breath. Thick saliva began to flood from his mouth. He twisted in his chair, opening his mouth and gaping upward toward the ceiling. Then suddenly he began to scream. Sitko lunged to restrain his brother as he tried to leap from his chair. There was a hushed confusion as the people in the restaurant pulled back in fear. Suddenly Reno fell down. Sitko tried to keep him on his feet, but he could not hold him up. He fell down, and when he struck the floor something inside him seemed to burst, and his body convulsed. Jemina gasped and fell to her knees over her son. Sitko tried to get Reno to his feet, but his brother's eyes had gone blank and blood was running from his nostrils.

"My God!" Jemina Ghost Horse was yelling. "Somebody help us! Please! Somebody help us! I think my son is dying! My God . . . my son is dying!"

Sitko could not stand the sound of his mother's screaming. He threw up his hands and thrashed the air. Everywhere was a blinding light. Everywhere he looked there were great, leaping flames. He was lost in the exploding light, spinning around and around until he came to rest in a hospital, where he stood, looking down at his brother.

Reno vomited. He yelled as vomit flew from his mouth. He thrashed to and fro as they strapped him to a table and shoved a wad of cotton between his teeth. Then they shot electricity through his brain. His body jolted for just a moment and then it turned to jelly. Sitko felt sick. The world was

149

on fire again. Everywhere there were great flames. Until suddenly the fire went out. And Reno was quiet.

He lay perfectly still in a tiny white room at the hospital, a vacant expression upon his solemn face. Sitko stayed with him day and night. But his brother did not seem to know him.

Then one day a man appeared at Reno's bedside. It was Jamie Ghost Horse.

Sitko had not seen his father in so many years that he didn't recognize him. He tried to recall the tall dark man he had seen weeping in the hallway of Star of Good Hope, but this man was not the same person. He was shorter now. He was thinner. The muscles on the left side of his face had collapsed and his features ran together. In his eyes was a terrible weariness.

He smiled meekly, looking first at Reno and then at Sitko. Then, after a short while, he turned and left.

Sitko stared after him, still unable to grasp that this man was his father. He felt anger and confusion and longing. How could he let him slip out of his life without saying a single word to this man who was his real father? And yet he simply could not speak.

A few days later Reno was discharged from the hospital. He looked at Sitko in silence as they took the long bus ride to the dusty little street where Sitko had found an apartment. Reno had changed. He was filled with a dark silence. Words passed between them slowly, as if they lived at a great distance from one another.

Reno sat in a big chair, looking out the window onto an ugly treeless street lined with crumbling bungalows. Sitko never left his brother except when he had to go to the market for food. When he ran out of money, Sitko called his mother.

"You know how Alexander feels about the two of you," she whispered over the phone. "If he thinks I'm giving you anything, he'll make a lot of trouble." She was silent for a long time. Then she said: "All right . . . all right. I can give you a few dollars, but God help us if Alexander finds out!"

"Where can I meet you?" Sitko asked.

"I can't leave the house. Your grandmother has been sick ever since Alexander threw you out, and I can't leave until the doctor comes."

"What should I do?"

"You'll just have to take a chance and come here for the money."

Sitko looked in on his brother to make certain he was comfortable. Then he hurried off to the house of Alexander Milas-Miller.

He did not know that Jamie Ghost Horse had been watching their apartment. He did not realize that his father was following him to the house of the man who had taken his wife and his sons.

Jamie Ghost Horse trailed after Sitko. He waited cautiously on the street, and then he crept up the long driveway and stood among the trees, watching as Jemina hurried out the kitchen door and pressed a wad of money into Sitko's hands.

When Sitko got back to the street, he noticed someone up near the house, standing among the bushes by the front door. He was thinking that the man was probably the gardener as he reached into his pocket for bus fare. Then for some reason he didn't get on the bus. The door hissed shut as he peered back at the house. Just then Alexander and Jemina came out of the front door. It was not until his mother had gotten into the car that Sitko realized that the figure hiding in the trees was Jamie Ghost Horse.

Alexander Miller saw him at the same moment. He ran at him, yelling a warning to Jemina. But Jamie leaped into the driveway in front of the car and stood there without moving. Once again Alexander shouted as Sitko began running up the driveway in hopes of convincing Jamie to leave in peace. Suddenly two shots resounded in Sitko's ears. Alexander Miller stumbled and fell down. Birds burst into flight, rising like a black cloud over the trees.

Sitko stopped abruptly and stared up the drive at the motionless body on the gravel. He froze as he watched Jamie Ghost Horse slowly circling the prostrate body of Alexander Miller and walking deliberately toward the automobile, where Sitko's mother sat without moving or making a sound.

Sitko shouted for him to stop, but nothing came out of his mouth. He watched in horror as Jamie opened the car door. Then he whimpered and felt sick as his father fired two shots into his mother's body.

His mother screamed. She screamed and screamed. He could never forget the sound of her screaming. At night he cried out when he heard echoes of his mother's voice, wailing all around him. He could bear the sound no longer. He spun around and ran headlong into the darkness until he could run no farther. Then he sobbed and fell into Patu's arms.

It was silent in the little prison. Sitko sat motionless against the whitewashed walls while Patu mopped the sweat from his face. He tried to catch his breath as his eyes blinked and he gazed around the room. Patu was talking, but he could hear nothing but the pounding of his pulse. Finally the walls took shape and Patu was saying, ". . . be calm . . . it is all right, Sitko Ghost Horse . . . it will be all right."

"Listen to me . . ." he murmured. "Listen to me."

"It is all right. You should not talk for a moment."

But Sitko needed to talk.

"Listen to me," he pleaded, clearing his throat and sitting upright against the wall. "I want to tell you about Jemina. I want you to know how it was when I came out of my mother's hospital room," Sitko gasped. "I remember that there were newspaper reporters in the hallway, just as there had been when Eric was hit. The reporters gazed with an unspeakable fascination at the blood that had poured down my shirt and jeans when I carried my mother out of the car and into the ambulance. I had seen exactly the same expression in people's eyes when I carried Eric into the emergency room. No sympathy . . . no sympathy. Just a terrible curiosity. The blood, you see, the blood fascinated them. And now all the blood flows together, and I cannot separate one thing from another. I remember that flashbulbs began to burst in my face. And they asked me about the rips in my jacket where someone had clutched at me and screamed in pain. Perhaps it was my mother or perhaps it was Eric. I no longer remember. I just remember that they offered me money to tell them exactly how the shooting had happened. They stood in my path and would not let me pass, though I was desperate to escape from them. But they wouldn't let me go, until at last an orderly shouted at them and pushed me into a linen closet, where I leaned senselessly against the wall and panted for breath in the darkness. Finally it was quiet in the corridor. I crept out of the closet and sat on a bench in the hallway. I stayed there all night. At six o'clock in the morning they came out of my mother's room and wheeled her toward the elevator and up to the operating room. When I asked if she was going to be all right, the nurse gave me a dark look, and I felt my insides dissolve. When the elevator door closed, I wandered down the halls until I found the room where Alexander Milas-Miller lay in a coma. A tangle of tubes hung in the air above his body. Bottles of yellow and white liquid bubbled as they fed the tubes droplets of fluids that flowed through needles in Alexander's arms. His mouth gaped but he did not seem to be breathing. I stood there astonished by the sight of him, until a nurse waved me away. 'Absolutely no visitors,' she said.

"I went back to the hall and waited. A constant procession of maimed and broken bodies passed by me, hour after hour. Women in wheelchairs. Men on crutches. Bodies on tables, wrapped in sheets. I could smell the pain. I could see it on the stunned faces of people who limped down the hall, their fragile bodies desperately scattered. I tried to think of something else. I recalled my grandmother and the marvelous courage in her eyes as she stood with a knife, ready to defend Reno and me against all the demons of the world. And then the doctor came to me and told me that my mother was dead."

"Ah . . ." Patu murmured as she sorrowfully rocked back and forth, her arms wrapped around her chest. "Such a terrible time for you, Sitko Ghost Horse. Such a difficult life for you. A terrible thing to lose the mother. And your friend? Your friend Eric . . . did he also die?"

"No," Sitko whispered. "The wounds from the glass did not kill him. It did something far worse than that. When he came out of the hospital he had changed. It was the same for

Eric as it had been for my brother. He was full of a dark silence. He wanted nothing to do with people. Not even me. We barely spoke anymore. He slept fitfully an hour at a time on the couch near his desk. He never again sat down with me at the dining table. He lived at a distance. Afraid to touch me. Unwilling to venture outside. Everything he had feared had happened to him. And there was no escaping the trouble. The whole thing was all over the newspapers. And somehow everybody seemed to know about it. They didn't want to know what really happened. That didn't interest them. And now nobody wanted my pictures anymore. People stopped coming to the studio. The fans and the friends disappeared. There was no mail. No phone calls. No invitations. No interviews. The press acted as if I no longer existed. And Suzanne pulled down my show. So that was that," Sitko said with a shrug. "I guess I should have done something when people first started the ugly stories. But it all seemed so stupid to me. So I ignored it. When you are successful, there are always people who hate you. And apparently I was a success, though I was the last to know it."

"What did they do, these enemies? Did they use bad magic? Did they make many bad things happen for you?"

"Yes, they made bad things happen."

"But why did they do these things?"

"I really don't know. I'm not sure if any of them really know why they did it. They knew nothing about me and I knew nothing about them. I guess they just needed a devil and for some reason I was it. I can't help wondering why it had to be me. I've tried to figure it out, but I don't have the answers. All I know is that there have always been people who have loved me too much and people who have detested

155

me. And so there have always been pain and death and vio-
lence. Somehow I can't seem to escape them."

It was after the death of his mother that Sitko left the house
of Alexander Milas-Miller. He embraced Grandma Amana
and left her at the door, where she stood tearfully waving after
him. But Sitko did not weep. There was nothing left inside
of him and he could no longer feel pain.

It was not until Sitko went to art school and met Eric Jones
that he rediscovered his feelings. And then he was happy for
a little while.

But one night a great white owl flew into their lives, and
the world caught fire once again. It was after the wounding
of Eric Jones that the white owl appeared in the darkness and
set the world on fire. And it was in the night of the white owl
that Sitko's friends began to die.

Looking back, Sitko could see the world enveloped in a
dense white fog. Gradually, everything vanished into the
vapors that tumbled down upon him. Now the empty night
was filled with inconsolable cries. Ten thousand tortured cats.
A piercing whine conveying an everlasting, inexpressible misery. Then the sky turned to silver dust that swirled upward in
the wind.

"What happened to you, Sitko Ghost Horse?" Patu urged.

Sitko didn't answer. He looked out the window of his
prison, into the darkness, recalling the fire leaping violently
and exploding with a roar of thunder as it tore a great hole in
the blackness.

Out of that fiery puncture came the huge white bird that
swooped down upon him, flapping its great jagged wings so

powerfully that the fire scattered. Instantly the world caught fire, and the flames leaped toward Sitko.

"Ah," Sitko whimpered as he searched into the smoke and fog. "Ah . . ." he moaned. A mysterious rush of wings silently swept across the ground at Sitko's feet. "It was an owl!" he muttered, his face full of fear. "It was an owl. . . ."

"What happened to you, Sitko Ghost Horse?" Patu urged.

Sitko didn't answer. He gazed out the window, into the blinding light that was consuming the darkness.

"What happened to you?" Patu asked again as she approached Sitko and gently shook him. But Sitko did not respond. He stood silently, gazing into the world beyond the window.

Patu nodded with concern. "Is that when you came into the desert?" she asked. "Is that when you left your people and came to our village?"

After a long silence, Sitko muttered: "No . . . later . . . it was later. When everyone was dying . . . from the sickness."

"Ah . . . *the sickness* . . ." Patu groaned, as if the very word were malignant.

THIRTEEN

Some are so young,
Some suffer so much . . .

—WALT WHITMAN, "THE WOUND-DRESSER"

IN THE CITY a cry of joy went up and there was laughter and celebration. It was Thanksgiving, the holiday that Sitko Ghost Horse most loved. It was the time of the harvest moon. The great feast day of renewal and hope and generosity. People who were usually caustic and unfriendly were full of smiles as they hurried from shop to shop, loaded down with bundles of lavish foods for the festive evening meal. For the moment, the city was congenial. Everyone smiled at passersby. But few people were friendly to Sitko Ghost Horse. The success that had transformed his life had completely vanished. And with the loss of that prosperity, Sitko had been faced by the endless and silent contempt of the same people who had once sought his friendship. His income had dwindled. He had no prospects. And he felt betrayed and abandoned. He could no longer be what he had spent his entire life becoming. He had changed. There was no longer a timid young man hidden inside of him. Now he was someone else, but he did not know for certain who he had become.

Sitko wandered among the jubilant people of his neighborhood, looking for familiar faces. But no one spoke to him. When he passed people he knew, their warm smiles faded and they turned away. A terrible depression began to overtake Sitko. How could the same people who declared themselves libertines and devoted friends be capable of believing ridiculous rumors? It was absurd. And it was depressing.

Sitko had come out to escape the gloom of his studio, where he could not get any work done as long as Eric sat listless and silent in a dark corner. But the mood was no better in the streets than it was at home. He was about to give up and go back to the studio when he caught sight of Frank Adams, one of their oldest friends. He shouted to him. "Hello, Frank! My God, we haven't seen you in weeks."

When Frank heard someone calling to him, his face lighted with friendliness. But the expression instantly withered when he recognized Sitko. For a moment he faltered. Then without speaking, he quickly crossed to the other side of the street and rushed away. The snub was so obvious that Sitko self-consciously glanced around to see if anyone had witnessed his embarrassment.

Sitko wanted to be by himself. In the shadows behind the abandoned factories he sat quietly and gazed out into the little square where a group of men were setting up a large Christmas tree. He smiled to himself as he watched them argue about how their task should be accomplished. Then he felt a curious motion in the air, and a deep, foul stench swept around him. In the darkness of the alley Sitko could see someone slowly coming his way. And it seemed to him that the distant figure smiled and beckoned to him. Then the pale person lifted his hand from his hip and pointed outward toward some immense and mysterious expectation. As the figure came nearer, Sitko made out a handsome young man dressed in strange clothes and ornaments. But the person changed again and again as he came closer. Upon the face of the young man was a thick white chalk that made him the color of the Moon. And under his nails were silvery crystals that glistened in the twilight. Though his body was very slender and his face exceptionally handsome, Sitko somehow dreaded this young man as he approached him slowly, limping slightly as if he were crippled. A deep shadow followed at his side, keeping him in perpetual obscurity.

"Good evening," the strange young man said in a toneless voice. "What is your name?"

"Sitko . . . Sitko Ghost Horse."

"And what are you doing sitting here alone in the dark while everybody else is having a good time?"

Sitko shrugged, not knowing how to answer. Then he peered closely into the young man's pale face and tried to discern his features in the deep shadows that surrounded him. As his eyes gradually became accustomed to the gloom, Sitko could see that countless sores covered the boy's handsome face. His skin was ruptured and rancid. Tiny white worms squirmed out of his nostrils, where they wiggled helplessly in the dim light of evening before they slithered back out of sight. His tangled black hair was matted with excrement, dried pus, and urine. And his eyes had no iris or color but were blank and milky white.

"Who are you and what are you called?" Sitko murmured fearfully.

The young man smiled unpleasantly and licked his putrid lips. "My name is Delito," he said tonelessly. "You do not yet

160

know me, but very soon you will meet me. I am a stranger to you. I came to your city with my friends, who are the people of the Moon. But they are gone, and they have left me behind."

"Ah," Sitko murmured in dread. "And what are you doing here?"

"I bring death," the young man said softly. "I will show you. Come sit near me, Sitko Ghost Horse," he cooed softly as he sighed and squatted upon the ground, loosening his pants and spreading his legs. "Come lie down beside me."

Sitko cringed as the young man's chalky hand reached toward him. He knew that if this dreadful creature embraced him he would surely die, yet he did not dare move away. Then the young man paused. His hideous hand remained poised in midair, close to Sitko's groin. He smiled slowly as he gazed at Sitko, but he did not touch him.

Sitko tried to give the appearance of friendliness while he searched his mind for some means of evading the terrible stranger.

"I am flattered," Sitko said with a frightened smile, "to be the one person of these thousands of people in the city with whom you wish to be friends."

"I have no favorites," the young man murmured as he gazed at Sitko's crotch. "I am always hungry for people. I desire everyone I see—little boys and old men, beautiful women and newborn babies."

"I am flattered," Sitko repeated self-consciously, "but I am such a pathetic fellow. Surely you don't want to bother with me. I am exhausted and I have no desire left in me. I have grown cold with sorrow and neglect."

"Then you will not lie down with me?" the young man asked darkly.

"Surely you would rather have one of the strong young men whose virility is praised by wives and lovers. Surely you would prefer a happy fellow and not someone like me," Sitko stammered.

"You are right!" the young man snapped with annoyance as he covered his face and withdrew. "I was only pitying you because you are lonely and unhappy. But if you will not come to me, there are many people on the streets, and I shall find far better welcome among them!"

Then he limped slowly toward the crowded square. The sweet odor of decay flew into the wind and followed after him. The obedient shadows trailed doggedly in his footsteps. And as he moved into the crowd he left a fragile trail of cinders and blood. Then he vanished, but the long twisted shadow that his body had cast upon the pavement lingered long after he had left, making a terrible blemish upon the earth.

It was on the night of Sitko's encounter with the hideous young man that people began to fall down and rave with fever. The sweat poured from their bodies. They could not breathe and they could no longer walk. They groaned and lay helplessly. The smell of decay came from their mouths when they collapsed. Purple bruises spread over their bodies, and their lungs filled with pus. They stumbled sightlessly as the light in their eyes went out. They raved and fell to the ground, seized by violent fits. And they stank as if they were already dead. The sickness was like a fire. It nibbled at the fingers of men and women and children. And then it laughed as it devoured their flesh and their minds. Their strong bodies shrank into sacks of bone. Fragile. Emaciated. Wasted. Cadaverous. Few people would attend the afflicted and few dared to touch them. And gradually they closed their hollow eyes, one by one, and then they died.

Just before Christmas, Sitko received news that Frank Adams was dead. A few days later, he heard that Suzanne had died. One by one, their friends began to die. A whole tribe of talented people.

Sitko and Eric watched death stampede across their world. They sat on the fire escape and looked down upon their neighborhood as familiar faces disappeared and fewer and fewer people walked along the street below. Now starving dogs wandered the alleys and wailed all night, their yellow eyes filled with madness. In alleys they growled and snapped and snarled as they fought one another and snatched at the abandoned corpses of children.

Sitko fearfully embraced Eric. "My God," he whispered, "we are so alone. There is hardly anyone left but the two of us. How lonely the world has become."

For a long time Eric sat silently, looking aimlessly down into the street. Then he said, "A lot I care. All of those bastards betrayed you! How can you care what happens to them? Where were they when we had our trouble? Where were the people you trusted and the people you encouraged and helped? Where was that asshole Frank? And how about Suzanne? Afraid of their own fucking shadows! Afraid to take a stand for fear of being tainted by sticking up for you. That's where they were!"

"None of that seems very important anymore," Sitko said. "Forget about it, Eric. I don't even think about it anymore. None of it made any sense, but it still scared the hell out of me. For a time, I really didn't think I would keep my sanity. But now the sickness has made a mockery of all those people and their foolishness. What does it matter now?"

Eric sighed heavily and touched Sitko's hand. "I wish I could let things go the way you do," he murmured. "I wish I didn't have to hate so much."

For the first time in many months, Eric looked into Sitko's eyes. "They are gone," he said. "And what remains of us? Not much, I fear. All our real friends have vanished. And soon there will be no one left but you and me. And what makes us worthy of surviving?"

"Let's at least be happy that we're both okay," Sitko said quietly. "We are still here, my friend. It's a miracle, when you think about it. Somehow we have survived all the bad days and we are here with one another. That is really something of a miracle. So whatever else happens, at least we have one another!"

Now Eric's dark face was filled with affection. For a long time he remained silent. Then he smiled, and, touching Sitko's shoulder, he said good night. He turned out all the lights in the studio, while Sitko stood silently in front of a canvas that had remained unfinished for several months. Now Eric slowly approached and stood next to Sitko, his arm hanging around his friend's shoulder. "Perhaps it's time for both of us to get back to work," he murmured.

"I think you're right," Sitko said.

Then Eric went to bed.

But Sitko could not sleep. He sat up in the darkness of the cavernous loft. His chest ached and he could not catch his breath. His every heartbeat frightened him. His every ache sent a shock of dread through him. *Could it be the sickness?* He

164

tried to think of something else. In the dark he tried to dream himself back into existence. He tried to dream about another day of life. But living in a dying world was more terrible than not existing at all. Each time news came of the death of someone he had known, he felt both sorrow for his friend and delight that he himself had survived. And then he would feel a terrible sense of guilt. Just for staying alive. For surviving while so many others were dead or dying. The air was filled with the names of people he had lost. Of love that was lost. Sitko closed his eyes and summoned his brother, Reno, and his mother, Jemina; he kissed Eric the way he had kissed him years and years before; and he saw his grandmother crouching patiently in a dark corner, waiting for the day when the lost world of her people would be found once again.

Now a frail glow crept slowly through the window. The neighborhood factories lurched into motion and soiled the morning. The studio was utterly silent. And in the silence, the fatigue and depression in Sitko's head spoke to him like an enemy. The voice in his mind frightened him. Each time he attempted to take a breath, he felt his heart throb, and a terrible panic flooded through him.

Then suddenly he sat up and cried out. He struggled to awaken, but sleep pinned him down like a great immovable weight. He stared into the dimness. Something had awakened him. Something in the darkness. There was a noise. Now the door of the loft slowly opened. Standing there in the dim light of morning was a huge white bird.

Sitko stumbled to his feet.

The light coming through the dirty windows turned yellow, and an automobile backfired in the street below. He snatched up a vase and spun around with a shout, throwing it with all his might. The vase smashed against the wall.

He trembled in the silence.

The owl had vanished.

Quickly, Sitko splashed some water on his face. Then he crept toward the kitchen. The loft was filled with shadows. In a panic, he quickly turned on all the lights.

Nothing. There was nothing there.

Now he looked in on Eric. He was still sleeping on the couch, curled up, with a pillow over his head. Sitko sighed with relief. To calm himself he made a cup of coffee and waited for Eric to get up. He sat in a daze at the kitchen table and waited a long time, until gradually the fear dissipated and his eyes dimmed from fatigue and he fell asleep.

When the sound of traffic awakened Sitko, he discovered that it was almost noon.

Where was Eric? Was he all right?

Sitko pressed his fingers to his temples, as if he had been struck hard against the head. For a moment he reeled, and then he leaned heavily against the table.

"Eric? Are you up?"

Sitko groaned with fear, and his voice rattled along behind him as he leaped to his feet and rushed to Eric. It was dark in the corner enclosed by towering shelves of books, and when Sitko peered through the dimness at Eric, he saw him still lying on the couch with his arms widely spread and a blank expression on his face.

"My God, but you gave me a fright!" Sitko said. "Do you know what time of day it is?" Sitko exclaimed as he turned on the light over Eric's desk.

For a moment, there was no response. Then Eric stirred and laboriously sat up, looking pale and feverish.

"What's the matter?" Sitko asked nervously, throwing open one of the large windows. "Are you all right?"

"Yes . . . yes. It's just my throat. I think maybe I swallowed something. It feels like I have something in my throat . . . like a fishbone or something."

In the steaming daylight Sitko saw a great wind rise and vanish into the sky. The sight frightened him.

"Let me take a look. Let me see. Sit up and open your mouth . . . this way . . . toward the light."

When Sitko looked into Eric's mouth he was astonished to see a thick white growth that completely covered Eric's throat and tongue.

"What do you think it is?" Eric asked.

Sitko was so fearful that he could not respond.

After two months of severe illness, Eric was still weak and feverish. Test after test provided no clue to what was wrong with him.

"Tell me honestly, doctor," Sitko anxiously asked when he took Eric to the hospital for tests. "Is it the sickness?"

"You have to stay calm," was the doctor's response. "Don't panic. After all, people can still be ill without having it."

Sitko tried to believe the doctor. But as the weeks went by he became increasingly alarmed. Eric had little energy and a constant temperature. The flulike congestion in his chest had finally subsided, but he was steadily losing weight. And the furry white infection in his throat persisted.

Sitko was becoming so frightened he could not sleep, but he kept his fear to himself. Eric became more and more sensitive and secretive about his illness, fearful of what people might think. He insisted that Sitko tell everyone that he was much better. When one of their few remaining friends visited the studio, Eric hid away in the bathroom so he wouldn't see him. He refused to go out for fear that neighborhood people would start to talk.

"Do you think I'm going to be okay?" Eric asked with concern, hoping for Sitko's reassurance.

"Of course!"

But Eric did not get better. A great sadness filled the studio. Until one morning when Eric got marvelous news. An editor who had asked to see one of his novels almost a year earlier finally called and said that his company liked the book and wanted to publish it. Despite everything, Eric was happier than he had been in a very long time. And though he still had little energy, he immediately started to work on the revisions.

"When you sign the contract," Sitko exclaimed, "I'm taking you to the best restaurant in town!"

The book contract came and was signed, but there was no celebration. Eric was ill once again. He did not have the strength to climb the four flights of steps to the studio. He sat listlessly at his desk, forcing himself to work. Despite his misery, he was filled with determination. But his energies were easily depleted. And after a short time at his typewriter, he slouched to his couch and lay listlessly, trying to catch his breath. Then he fell asleep. When he awakened he was covered with sweat. He coughed violently, hardly able to speak. He tried to eat the soup that Sitko prepared for him, but it wouldn't stay down. He staggered to the bathroom and crouched on the floor in front of the toilet, vomiting thick, foamy mucus. Sitko held his head while he vomited, and mopped his face. He shuddered as he watched what was happening to Eric's beautiful body and handsome face. It seemed as if he were dissolving, bit by bit.

Then, just a few weeks before his thirty-fifth birthday, Eric collapsed as he was working at his desk. An ambulance was summoned and he was rushed to the hospital.

When Sitko was admitted to his room, Eric lay unconscious and pale, his arms strapped to the railings of the bed. A large plastic tube was jammed into his mouth and ran down into his throat. His eyes were taped closed. A narrow feeding tube had been inserted into his nostril. His lips were bruised and swollen. His forearms were streaked with long black and yellow contusions, where a dozen needles had pierced the skin. Another large tube ran from under the white sheet covering him. It flowed into a transparent plastic bag that was gradually filling with bloody urine.

Sitko stood by the bed, numb with fear. Overwhelmed by the sight of Eric's tormented body. The only sound was the unrelenting hiss and mechanical pulse of a machine that pumped air into his friend, moment by moment.

That night Eric almost died. By morning, however, his condition had finally stabilized. Then miraculously, with each day, Eric's health began to improve. But Sitko remained deeply troubled.

"It's a roller coaster," the doctor said. "You never know from day to day."

But Eric continued to improve. And eventually the doctor announced that Eric was sufficiently recovered to go home.

"Given the nature of his illness, it's impossible for anyone to know what will happen or how long he will survive.

I'm sorry, but I can't give you much hope."

A nurse handed Sitko a large box filled with bottles of pills. She smiled weakly and gave him a sympathetic look. "It's going to be a bit of a chore for you."

Sitko distractedly thanked the woman as he looked with bewilderment at the dozens of bottles of pills.

"Now take Eric home," she murmured with a grave expression that wilted Sitko's hope. "And try to help him enjoy his life while it lasts. . . ."

The words stung. Tears came into Sitko's eyes. And he quickly turned and hurried down the hall to where Eric awaited him, sitting helplessly in a wheelchair.

An orderly wheeled Eric to the hospital entrance, where Sitko found a taxicab. Then they carefully lifted Eric and placed him on the backseat. As he took his friend into his arms, Sitko was horrified by the fragility of Eric's body. There was little left of him. His pelvis protruded from his sides. The muscles had vanished from his torso. His bony knees were larger than his thighs. And he barely had the strength to lift his arms.

Sitko tried to smile, but he could not do so. He pulled his hands away from Eric's shriveled body. He turned his head and bit down hard on his lip. He tried not to think about the past. *White moonlit nights . . .* He tried not to remember how things used to be. *Sleeping on the river's bank.* He dreaded memories more than anything else. But they pursued him. *The handsome dark face. The fine body, sleek as sculpture.* He feared that Eric would see the remorse in his eyes. But all his efforts were in vain. He slipped slowly backward, into the deep summer, followed by a glorious light. Moonlight. The river in moonlight. The river in moonlight on a summer's night . . . stretching out in the heat that loomed just above the luminous earth. A spider . . . twisting on its glowing thread, dangling upside down and slowly moving its long back legs in an endless succession of gestures, conjuring silver out of nothing. Sitko looked up at the smoke that ringed the great yellow Moon. The river resounded all around. Leaf patterns fell upon them, speckling their youthful bodies with shadow. Eric turned slowly, and the image of branches wove an ornamental lacework across his dark muscular thighs. And slowly they retreated into each other's bodies, limb upon limb. He was shining. Like something freshly dug from the earth. He smelled of berries and horses. He was as sleek as a colt. And he was beautiful. They laughed. The river spread out in the moonlight as they laughed. And then they rolled slowly into the deep, wet grass. They came together hesitantly, filling the space between them softly, slowly, until the Moon disappeared behind their closed eyes and the grass began to sing its long green song. Now even the spider had vanished, abandoning its luminous silver trellis in midair.

Sitko carried Eric up the stairs to the loft. And then he put him to bed. Exhausted and listless, Sitko sat on a kitchen chair and stared into the darkness.

Now the sickness was always on Sitko's mind. He could not paint. When he spent time trying to work, his thoughts constantly wandered off—focusing upon the absurdity of Eric's situation, the stupidity of death and dying, and the utter helplessness he felt.

As the weeks passed, Sitko tried not to be resentful about what was happening to his own life. But it was difficult. Interest in his career was slowly beginning to revive, but he found it impossible to paint. He could not work and he could not keep appointments with gallery owners. He had to stay with Eric. He would have been able to live without any time for himself, if only Eric had shown some recognition of the situation and said something about it. But he said nothing. And now he had turned inward upon his illness and his own mortality to such an extent that he had left Sitko to deal with everything else.

Things finally improved as Eric regained his energy. He took over some of his own needs, making life less hectic for Sitko. One sunny Sunday morning, they cautiously made their way down the stairs to the street, where Eric treated Sitko to brunch at a café in the neighborhood. They talked about things that neither of them had mentioned for months. About travel and books and music. They laughed and smiled at one another as they had tea with milk, scones, and marmalade. It was their first outing in more than a year.

With his renewed health, Eric was obsessively working on the revisions of his novel. But he constantly overextended himself and found himself back in bed, unable to get up. There were some good days, but most of them were bad. Sitko tried to keep Eric's spirits up, but the quality of his life was miserable, and his chances of surviving were not good. Though all of his trouble, Eric was wonderfully brave. Sitko greatly admired his courage and stamina as he watched his friend try with all his will to get a few things accomplished each day. He sat with great determination at his typewriter trying to work, but he could only complete a few sentences before having to stagger back to bed.

For Sitko it was not easy to watch his friend in such a state. It broke his heart. Sometimes he locked himself into the bathroom so Eric would not see his panic and grief.

Now Sitko sat at his easel stupefied by his inability to paint. The atmosphere in the studio was stultifying. He felt as if the world were coming to an end. The silence was deadening. The telephone rarely rang and the mail withered away. He would have considered it a blessing not to have to answer a lot of calls and mail, but under the circumstances he had the strangest feeling that he was slowly disappearing. To cheer himself and in order just to accomplish something, he lined the walls of the studio with the paintings he had done for his last show at Suzanne's gallery. Now, while Eric slept, he sat on the floor in the middle of the loft, drinking a bottle of red wine and looking intently at his pictures. Somehow they disgusted him. Perhaps it was their sexual images that repulsed him. The sexuality of the paintings, which had seemed so naive and natural to him a year earlier, now appeared utterly deadly and grotesque. And gradually, as Sitko became drunk, he solemnly recognized that he had come to think of the human body as a monstrous malignancy.

The next morning, Eric could not get out of bed. When Sitko brought his breakfast, tears suddenly came to Eric's eyes.

Sitko called the doctor and begged him to see Eric. But the doctor's voice was hoarse and weak.

"I'm sorry to do this to you, Sitko. I have been sick for the last week. If I feel better, I'll continue to treat Eric, but it's difficult to say what will happen. I have been trying to find another doctor to look after Eric, but most physicians are afraid to treat people with the sickness."

The doctor's health continued to deteriorate, but, somehow, within a week, Eric was back on his feet. His determination to live was staggering. He completed work on his novel, which his editor praised. And now, at last, he became less obsessed with work.

"At least I've published one book in my life!"

So he began to relax as he tried to enjoy another recovery, no matter how brief. With renewed energy he did everything he could do to make life easier on Sitko.

"Sit . . . sit . . . sit!" Eric ordered playfully. "Dammit, it's my turn to play the parlor maid!"

Sitko was able to have some time for himself. And even his career was brightening. A gallery offered to give him a show. He was delighted, but he was also reluctant to open himself and his work to attack. Once he had sought the attention of the public. Now he was no longer certain that the praise of a few people was worth the rage of those who envy and detest celebrity. But a young painter he admired persuaded him to accept the show. "Times have changed," the young man told him. "Nobody is going to be offended by things like that. If I were you I wouldn't worry about a few deadbeats who have it in for you. I saw the show at Suzanne's gallery and it was terrific. Believe me. You really should get those paintings back out in front of the public."

As news of Sitko's new exhibition spread, a magazine asked him for an interview. Sitko hedged, for fear of being set up for another scandal, but when the journalist expressed genuine interest in his painting, he was delighted to talk to him. Eventually the same newspaper that had attacked him as a fraud published an enthusiastic review of the exhibition. Nothing made sense, but Sitko was feeling strangely happy, despite Eric's illness. Having survived everything during all the bad years gave him a peculiar sense of satisfaction. But most important to him was the fact that Eric was still alive and getting the recognition he had always wanted.

Eric's novel had been released with great success. Now and again, when Eric felt well enough to go out, they went to a party, and Sitko happily lingered in a corner and watched Eric, who though pale and desperately thin was talking enthusiastically with people who had read his book and admired it. Sitko didn't want anything to ruin this rare triumph for his friend. He wanted to do something special for Eric. So despite the protests of his ailing doctor, they announced that they were going to visit the river resort where they had met. The doctor reluctantly arranged for Eric to have a blood infusion, which greatly increased his energy, and then Sitko and Eric packed and set out on a holiday.

It was glorious at the river, brilliantly sunny and clear and warm. Then, quite suddenly, Eric frowned and pressed his hand to the back of his neck. He made a little cry of pain, and something inside of him seemed to snap. He looked around in confusion, as if he did not know where he was. Then he turned very pale as fear overtook him.

"Ah . . ." he groaned, as his stomach turned and he whispered that he feared he was going to get sick in public. They hurried back to their cottage, where Eric fell to the floor before Sitko could get him into bed.

All the way to the airport Eric babbled senselessly about foreign soldiers he feared would shoot down the plane. For brief moments he seemed to recognize Sitko, but then he would pull back in horror as if he believed his friend might harm him. Sitko was desperate to get Eric quietly in his seat on the airplane, fearing that a flight attendant might recognize the symptoms and refuse to let someone with the sickness on board. Somehow they managed to get seated, and Sitko anxiously waited for the plane to take off.

Once they were in the air, Eric's teeth began to chatter and his body shook as he was overcome by a chill. Sitko covered him with blankets and tried to comfort him. But nothing seemed to help.

When they finally landed, Sitko requested a wheelchair and managed, with the help of a porter, to get Eric into a taxicab.

It was snowing, and traffic was backed up for miles. Eric's condition steadily worsened. When they finally reached the hospital, interns rushed to the taxi. Eric was taken to the emergency room. And then Sitko fell into a chair, exhausted, trembling. He sat without moving for hours. Eventually his eyes closed and he dozed off.

In the middle of the night he found himself looking into the light blue eyes of a young doctor.

"How do you feel?" the doctor asked.

Sitko tried to sit up, but his body would not awaken. "At night," he stammered, "at night, I sometimes wake up and when I look at Eric, his eyelids are swollen and his lips are discolored and cold. He mumbles, saying that he has demons with long pointed beaks sucking his blood. Every night he has dreams. And I am in his dreams. Is there no remedy for such dreams?"

The doctor did not answer. His figure became dim and distant, and Sitko reached out for him.

"I have seen Eric lying with open eyes," Sitko murmured. "When I watch him, something seems to crawl over him. It is nothing, not even a nightmare, and yet it is so dreadful that every limb of his body cries out. Can someone perish while he is still alive? Like a silk handkerchief devoured by moths? Can someone die of dreams? Can someone die while he is still alive and dreaming?"

"What are you trying to say?" the doctor asked as he shook Sitko by the shoulder.

Sitko leaped up with a shout, trembling and cold. It was still dark. Blinding darkness. There was nothing but the candle of his mind, flickering horribly, like a living thing spying on his sleep.

He could not speak. He just stared into the doctor's blue eyes.

"I'm sorry if I frightened you," the doctor was saying, "but I have news about your friend. I'm afraid he's very ill."

"What . . . what?" Sitko stammered.

"We have him on medication, and he can stay here over-night, but we are terribly overcrowded and I'm afraid that we can't keep him here more than tonight."

"What are you saying? What does that mean? Why can't you keep him here?"

"I'm sorry. But every bed is filled. There are people dying on the floor in hallways. We simply can't cope with any more patients. There are too many sick people," the doctor muttered exhaustedly. "We'll look after your friend tonight. That's truly the best we can do. Tomorrow you will have to take him home. He'll be more comfortable at home."

Now Eric's mind was being slowly devoured by the sickness. He thrashed about and groaned as he tried to get out of bed. Eventually he had to be restrained with straps. Now he lay pinned down, wide-eyed and panting, trying to suck air into failing lungs, surrounded by a terrible stench. His body could no longer fight the sickness. And there was nothing Sitko could do.

He unbound his friend's arms and massaged his bruised wrists. He leaned over the bed and wiped the sweat from his forehead. Eric opened his eyes and grappled for Sitko's hand. Then he raised it to his lips and kissed it. Sitko turned away, fearing that he would fall apart in front of his friend.

All night Eric gasped and groaned. All night Sitko watched and waited.

The next day Eric could not speak or focus his eyes. Sitko called the emergency room and begged for someone to come to the studio.

"If we can spare someone, we'll send a nurse over in a couple of hours."

Sitko placed his palms on Eric's chest. His pallid skin was tightly stretched over bare bones. His pulse was racing, and each breath took immense effort. Blood was seeping from between his lips. He was barely alive, trembling with fading pulsations of life. His face was unrecognizable, the handsome features melted away, leaving naked bone protruding from spotted flesh.

Sitko turned away and tried to contain himself. He could not bear to look at Eric's eyes. They had receded into his skull, draped with sagging black lids and filled with horror.

At midnight the nurse finally arrived, exhausted and anxious. She took one look at Eric and shook her head. "It's no good. No good . . ." she murmured. "I'm sorry."

Then she turned to leave.

"He's drowning! My God, he's suffocating. I can't stand to see him like this!"

She pressed a packet of morphine suppositories into Sitko's hands. "This will help," she whispered. "He is so weak and his body weight is so low, just one of them will put him to sleep. I don't know how you feel about things like this," she said with tears in her eyes. "But there comes a time . . ." Then she embraced Sitko and left without saying anything more.

Now Sitko was alone. Nothing remained but Eric and the morphine. Sitko opened his mouth wide and gulped for air like someone about to be forever submerged. Then he shrugged with bewildered resolve. He shook his head in disbelief as he stared down at the packet of morphine. There was no time left. They had run out of everything.

So, this was the end. Eric's suffering filled every corner of the studio like a long, brittle scream. An inconsolable, high-pitched whine that conveyed an inexpressible misery. The world had become unbearable. But none of that helped Sitko comprehend the necessity of what he had to do. He had rehearsed this moment in his mind so often, but still, as Eric's death approached none of those preparations were of any avail. He told himself that Eric was already dead despite his body's desperate efforts to survive. Now all that remained was Sitko. And he was trying with all his effort to hide from himself. Because he knew that when this nightmare was over, and he could no longer put all of his thoughts and energies and efforts into saving Eric, then the barriers holding back his sorrow would suddenly burst. And he would not be able to stand against the onrush of the tide. Surely he would break into a million pieces and drown in the torrent.

Standing over Eric with the morphine in his hands, he became more and more deeply aware of the impact the last few years had had upon him. He could feel the deepening cracks in his endurance. The agony of the plague, the stupidity and ruin of the scandal, and now Eric's death. These things had greatly dimmed and deadened his spirit.

And yet, now it was time to play God. Sitko Ghost Horse could not accept that role. He was ashamed of his inability to do what had to be done. But still he could not do it. And so he wandered away from Eric's suffering, slowly walking through the studio, still clutching the morphine in his hand. He gazed at the desk where Eric had worked. At the couch where he had slept. At the empty easel and the dusty tubes of paint, left untouched for such a long time. And then he went out onto the fire escape and sat staring into the moonlight.

Now nothing remained but a cascade of fantastic images that churned through the memory of Sitko Ghost Horse. The past begged to be remembered. It cried out to him. The people and the names. But nothing remained.

The house of Alexander Milas-Miller stood against the sky. The day had ended in a perpetual flood of moths. The windows of this great house were closed and dark now. No one entered and no one departed. Now there were no lights, no radios, no angry voices. Everyone had left the solemn house to face the night alone.

The blue-and-white morning glories had retreated for the night. They would not bloom again. The grass had turned gray. And the night collected itself into deep shadows among the bushes where the footprints of Jamie Ghost Horse had filled with rain.

Weeds began to grow in the graveled driveway where Alexander Milas-Miller's blood left its blemish. Jamie Ghost Horse laughed in a distant town and shouted to the bartender for another drink. The narrow door that flies open to the dead was always ajar in Gallup, New Mexico. Somehow that old man who was the father of Sitko and Reno vanished into his own massive death. Now what remained was an everlasting screech of brakes.

Jamie Ghost Horse walked out of the bar and staggered into his one-eyed pickup truck. Somewhere on the old road between Gallup and Albuquerque he drifted aimlessly into the wrong lane, gazing into the wondrous illumination that was coming toward him. There was a great explosion. And then silence. Now he was fast asleep within his tomb of twisted metal and shattered glass, beyond the reach of the policemen who had hunted him for years.

And so the night hovered over the house of Alexander Milas-Miller, who put aside his revolver and sat silently with his new wife in the dark dining room.

Occasionally a little man led prospective buyers across the lawn, but they never returned. People were as alien to this old house as love and happiness. Beneath the oak tree a stone still marked the place where Jamie threw down his gun and escaped into the street below. And sometimes when it was very quiet, passersby could hear the curious chanting of a crazy old woman who still lived in the room behind the kitchen. But no one listened to her songs.

Reno Ghost Horse smiled his bizarre smile when he enlisted in the Marines, lying about his illness. One day after leaving basic training, he died in the crash of a transport plane.

Nothing remained now but the long, retreating day. Weary of the world, the house of Alexander Milas-Miller had closed its windows and drawn its blinds. The stairway creaked, though feet rarely ascended to the second floor, where bedrooms were still kept immaculately prepared for guests who did not arrive.

Alexander Milas-Miller groaned with pain as he flopped into his big chair. He stared into space and mumbled nothing in particular. Sometimes he slept, but he never went upstairs to bed anymore. His wife sat beside him and watched in silence, while from the room behind the kitchen came the chanting of Grandma Amana as she made imaginary bead-work and chattered in a garbled language to Sitko's pictures on the walls.

No one turned on the lights anymore. No one disturbed the sheet-covered furniture. No one called. No one knocked. Nothing happened here anymore. Until one hot Sunday afternoon, when Alexander Milas-Miller slowly hunched over a glass of water and swallowed a fistful of pills. When it was almost dark they found him bobbing lifelessly back and forth in his chair, his arms thrown back, his robe open to reveal the deep blue scars upon his belly and urine slowly trickling down his white, hairless legs.

Grandma Amana shouted and fell to the floor, a bit of imaginary beadwork still clutched in her brown, wrinkled hand. The doctor was summoned, and she was put to bed.

Night was coming. Grandma Amana tried to fill her lungs as she mumbled the names of long-forgotten friends. You could hear the names all around, humming in the trees as Grandma Amana called out to them. Then she smiled peacefully at Sitko, who sat by her bed day and night, working feverishly to paint all the memories that poured from her. "I will keep you alive in my pictures," he pledged as Grandma Amana spun the marvelous tapestry of her life in the night air.

A spider crept undisturbed across the windowpane. But nothing else moved. Nothing happened. Nothing began or ended.

Yet in a Chinese garden, in brittle soil in some distant time and place, under fragrant eucalyptus trees where children often played, a herd of brilliant sweet peas rose high above the ground. No water flowed to nourish them. No hands extracted the weeds that strangled them. But miraculously they had survived, making their tortuous way through the hard, ungiving earth and climbing high into the air. Now in this longest night their blossoms poured a heavy honey into the air.

In her bed Grandma Amana was awakened by the fragrance of the flowers. Slowly she reached out to touch the animal that waited beside her bed, and then the beadwork tumbled from her hand.

A flood of smoky sunlight poured down on the fire escape, arousing Sitko from his troubled sleep. Still holding the morphine in his hand, he staggered to his feet, feeling stiff and cold. Now he was ready. He turned back into the studio and walked resolutely to Eric's bed.

His friend lay in the dimness. His eyes were wide, fixed in an expression of amazement. His mouth was open.

Sitko shuddered as tears flowed down his cheeks. He

leaned over his friend and touched his bony little arms still clutched across his chest. They were stiff and clammy and cold. A lifeless cold like no other cold.

He gazed steadily into his friend's face. And then, at last, he turned away and walked to the window.

Sitko Ghost Horse looked into the blinding light. The world was on fire. Everywhere he looked there were great, leaping flames. An enormous blast of light that spread across the land, devouring everything in its path. A horse with its mane ablaze raced along the horizon, disappearing into a cloud of smoke. Dogs were piled in smoking heaps. Everywhere there were burning corpses and smoldering automobiles. The air was filled with rumbles and roars. Explosions shook the walls as the fire obliterated the night, turning the sky fierce and white. The stars were on fire, and yet the wind that flew into his face was frigid and wet. The gigantic flames sent up a torrent of violent white light, and yet he could not feel the heat.

Looking back into the light, he could still hear the sound of people, crying out in anger and agony as they ran through the city setting fire to the piles of corpses that littered the streets. They were dressed in rubber suits, with yellow gloves and goggles and surgical masks. They clamored through the streets, yelling and cursing as they burned the dead. They went from house to house, dragging away the bodies, and then they set fire to the buildings.

Sitko peered into the light. Watching as the fire obliterated his world. As buildings bent and twisted in the heat. As his loft burst into flames and hundreds of blazing books fell from their shelves and cascaded onto the desk where Eric had worked. The books bounced and blazed as they flew in every direction, spreading out into a fiery heap on the floor. Sitko walked through the flames, climbing onto the fire escape. Everywhere he looked there were flames. Everything was burning. Garbage cans and neon signs. Animals and people. Boutiques and galleries.

Sitko stared into the firestorm. Watching silently as the wide windows of the gallery burst and exploded upward in a shower of crystal splinters. At once a huge ball of fire roared through the broken windows, bursting into the large white space where his paintings hung, as fragile and vulnerable as butterflies in a furnace. The canvases buckled in their frames. The colors winced in the heat, arching back and catching fire. Slowly the pigments loosened from faces and trees and mountains. Then, in a moment, the paintings were gone. The walls collapsed outward. And the air was filled with smoke.

It was on the night when the sky caught fire that Sitko Ghost Horse left the city far behind. He aimlessly drove into the desert until he ran out of gasoline. It was night, and he staggered into the darkness until he was confronted by people like none he had ever seen before. They seized him and would not let him go. He struggled against the ropes that restrained him. He fell to the ground and clung to the underbrush as they dragged him through the smoldering grassland. He fought against them until he fainted from pain and exhaustion.

Then he opened his eyes and found that he was a prisoner in a little room. And as he looked into the darkness beyond the window of his prison, all he could hear was a long lament. Even here and now, still he could hear nothing but the desperate cries of people. Somewhere out there. Beyond the world. From everywhere in the dark . . . there was still the inconsolable howl of frightened people. Weeping.

Weeping.

F O U R T E E N

▲

A GREAT STORM rolled down upon the desert. Black billowing
clouds flew out of the east, hovering like immense vultures
over the desolate village and turning the morning sky dark.
Streaks of lightning blistered the heavens. And the walls of the
little prison quaked as thunder shook the world.

Sitko sat upon the floor. Waiting. He had not slept. His
mind was filled with too many expectations and forebodings.
He dreaded closing his eyes for fear of the painful images that
would appear again and again in his dreams. And so he
waited, listening to the thunder. Soon Patu would bring his
food. Perhaps she would also have news from the elders.

Sitko sat apprehensively upon the ground and waited. He
listened for footsteps, for voices. But the rumbling in the sky
obliterated every other sound. It should have been day, but it
was night. The clouds blotted out the sun. And the desolate
land was smothered in a gray half-light. Thunder shouted in
the distant mountains, and the peaks momentarily blazed with
white light as the sky was ripped by lightning.

For a moment there was a deep silence, and then there was a piercing crack and the long bellow of the thunder. Another tremendous flash of light. And suddenly the darkness returned. Day turned to night. And Sitko no longer knew one day from another. All the days collided with one another, leaving a wide smear of time vaguely imprinted in his mind, without dates or times or places. The walls of his prison became increasingly familiar, until he began to feel secure in their shelter. He wanted to lie down. He wanted to stop thinking and give up. But the memory of his grandmother would not let him give in to defeat. He forced himself to think about freedom and life. He imagined being in some bright clean city by the ocean, where the people were still robust and friendly. He dreamed about having a new studio filled with light and music. How much he wanted to hear music! And how desperately he wanted to paint! To do all the things that he had not been able to do since Eric became sick . . . since he became a prisoner of this little room. He wanted to talk to people. He wanted to laugh. But most of all, he wanted to live. All at once, as the walls shook with the roar of thunder, he realized for the first time in months how desperately he wanted to live.

At first he had been paralyzed by fear of the sickness. From the time of the scandal and the coming of the sickness, Sitko had no longer cared what happened to him. The world had stopped. Nothing mattered. Nothing made any sense. And all his aspirations seemed utterly ridiculous. He had no desire to work. His career was over. His life was over. And he could no longer recall his reasons for wanting to be alive. Nothing was left of his world. The whole city was turning into a graveyard. The dead were everywhere. One by one, the people he loved vanished, leaving hardly a trace of their lives. The most beautiful dead.

But then, just when he thought he had nothing left to lose, he had been captured and he became a prisoner. And then, quite suddenly, Sitko knew that he urgently wanted to survive. He was no longer afraid of the plague. He was driven by it. Even if he could not survive, he vowed that he would make something of death even as he was dying. That frail idea of *freedom* grew more and more urgent as the thunder pounded down upon his prison and a hard rain began to fall. He stood at the window, looking out into the cascade of water pouring from the sky. More than anything in the world, he wanted to be free. He wanted to be out there in the pounding rain.

He could think of nothing else but freedom.

Surely they would let him go. They could not keep him captive forever. Soon the elders would have to decide what to do with him. And then, of course, they would set him free. Sitko was certain that any other decision was impossible. No matter how strange his predicament, he ardently believed that the elders would have to come to their senses and let him go.

Life without freedom was not enough. He was overcome with hopelessness as he watched the rain pouring down in such a torrent that it rebounded from the brittle soil. The earth had turned to concrete, as slick and hard as a culvert. And suddenly the desert was swept by a deluge that raced across the dusty land and burst against the walls of his prison and rushed under the door. Sitko snatched up his colors and the one remaining piece of cardboard. And then he climbed to the safety of the ledge and perched there as water flooded his cell.

Now, over the roar of the thunder, Sitko heard a noise. The door was unbolted and slowly swung open. Unfamiliar faces peered in at him. Then two priests slowly entered the room and looked at Sitko with an expression so filled with anger that he cringed and pressed his body against the wall.

Their wet bodies were covered with white and black paint that formed wide bands on their naked torsos and limbs. Around their chests they wore short capes made of animal skins, and on their heads they had headdresses with one long and arching horn.

The priests whispered to one another, but they did not speak to Sitko. After a moment, they waded through the flooded prison and approached Sitko as if they intended to take him away. But just as they were tying his hands and putting a rope around his neck, Patu appeared at the door and shouted at them.

They responded with angry voices and threatening gestures, flashing a long knife. But Patu stood her ground, and eventually the One Horn Priests backed away, snarling and pawing the air like lions subdued by a lion tamer.

When the One Horn Priests had left, Patu sighed with a mixture of relief and sorrow. Her face was troubled and she did not look Sitko in the eye.

"Fools are always in a hurry," she muttered. "I am sorry, Sitko Ghost Horse. I am sorry I did not come to you sooner, but I did not know that Delito had given you to the One Horns."

"What are you saying?" Sitko exclaimed. "Why are they here?"

"It is their duty," Patu said. "Now it is their duty to guard you."

"But why the One Horn Priests? You told me they kill people!"

"Yes," Patu said slowly, looking into Sitko's face and touching him lightly on the arm, "that is what I told you. They kill people."

Sitko's breath came in short gasps. He nodded with fear and confusion. And then his expression became blank and he felt numb as he realized what was happening to him.

"Ah . . ." he whispered in dread. "Then it is true. They have decided to kill me. . . ."

Patu did not speak. She merely nodded sorrowfully.

The two friends were silent as they looked at one another. Now there was no sound except the pounding of the rain and the rushing of the floodwaters. For a long time they stood helplessly, knee-deep in the water, unable to speak.

"So," Sitko sighed with a trace of anger and irony, "it would seem that we have come to the end of this ridiculous situation." He gave a dry laugh and shook his head in disbelief. "Absurd . . . what an absolutely absurd way for things to end!"

Again Patu nodded sadly as she murmured: "Yes."

Sitko covered his face. His mind so filled with thoughts and feelings that he felt as if he were drowning. There seemed to be nothing more for him to say. He looked up at Patu and shrugged with a childlike confusion, dumbfounded by the finality of the situation. "They have judged me . . . these men who do not know me. They have judged and condemned me." And again he laughed, as if he were scoffing at himself.

Patu spoke slowly. "I do not know . . . how to say what I must say to you, Sitko Ghost Horse," she faltered as tears flowed into her eyes. "I was thinking a long time about this.

191

About the Night of the Washing of the Hair. And about you. And about this village and my people. But I do not know how I can say to you what I am thinking."

Sitko sighed remorsefully as he put his hands on each of Patu's shoulders and smiled a weak smile. "Don't be so unhappy, my friend, or you will surely break my heart," he said softly, somehow feeling the need to console her. "We did our best, you and I. We tried to be something that people don't want us to be. And we tried to cross the great distance between us that they do not want us to cross. We risked everything, and somehow we have lost. But think of it! It was a fine idea, my friend. It must take a very great light to make such a deep shadow. That seems to be the way it is. We would like to deny it, but it always comes down to the same thing. We like to believe that something good comes out of our troubles. But inevitably we find out that it is the calamity itself that drives us. That's what makes us who we are. We are creatures on the brink of time, slipping into oblivion, hanging on the edge of extinction. And yet we think that our little lives go on for an eternity. Even as we slip away in time, we insist that our faces and voices and fragile bodies will endure, like mountains."

Sitko made a sound filled with remorse. And then he shrugged in dismay. "But, my friend, that is not the way it is. We are made of very fragile stuff. And time is hungry for us. It devours us and spits out our precious bodies, scattering our lives across the bottom of a wide sea of fantasy and expectation. Time eats us and licks our memories clean. And when the feast of time is over, all that remains is the piled bones of a person's whole world, blotted out and lost. All we have known and all we have said and done, all we have built, all we have created, all the ideals for which we have fought, and all the people we have loved sink beyond reach to the bottom of a vast sea of dream and memory."

The rain fell in deluges. Sitko and Patu stood looking out the window. The land was lighted by rapid bursts of blistering lightening.

"I want you to take this . . ." Patu whispered as she gently pressed the food bowl into Sitko's hands. "Please take this small offering from me."

Sitko grasped the bowl and nodded without speaking.

"Once I told you about this clay bowl. I told you it is a living thing. And so it is a life that I am giving to you, Sitko Ghost Horse," she said. "It is a creature made from the earth. It is made from the heart of the land. Just listen to it singing," she urged, pressing the bowl to Sitko's ear.

Sitko listened. The sound was like the hushed voice inside a seashell. He smiled as he heard the soft, persistent song of his own blood coursing through his body, echoing again and again from within the hollow of the bowl.

"I give you this bowl," she said softly. "It is all I have to give you, Sitko Ghost Horse. But it is alive. I want you to carry it when they take you away. I want it to go with you wherever you go. Will you do this for Patu?"

Sitko nodded.

Then Patu took the bowl from his hands and placed it carefully on the ledge. With one quick blow she drove the point of a small stone through the bottom of the bowl.

"What are you doing?" Sitko exclaimed. "Ah . . . you have broken it."

Patu raised the bowl into the air, peering at the small hole she had punctured in it. "No," she said. "It is a kill hole, my

193

friend. This bit of clay is a living creature from the earth. And now I have killed it. Now the spirit of the bowl is free to go with you. Now both the bowl and you, my friend, are free at last."

PART III: RETURN

"THE END"

We cannot express the light in nature because we have not the Sun. We can only express the light we have in ourselves.

—Arthur Dove

FIFTEEN

▲

With failing eyes K. could still see the two of them,
cheek leaning against cheek, immediately before his face,
watching the final act. "Like a dog!" he said; it was as
if he meant the shame of it to outlive him.

—FRANZ KAFKA

IT WAS IN the evening, when a fearsome silence fell upon the
world, that the One Horn Priests came to the prison of Sitko
Ghost Horse. They did not speak as they stood in the doorway, performing ritual movements, watching Sitko cautiously as if they feared him.

"So you have come," Sitko said flatly, standing up and
scrutinizing the priests with a mixture of curiosity and dread.

Still they did not speak. They quickly repeated their ritual,
which seemed to be used to ward off evil. Then they stepped
forward and bowed first to one another and then to Sitko. It
was a peculiar little movement, and despite his desperation
Sitko could not refrain from grinning, particularly since the
One Horn Priests, at close view, were more comic than
frightening. They were old men. Their naked bellies were
pendulous and soft. Layers of flesh hung from flabby arms.
And their faces, though made up to be terrifying, were rather

ordinary. Again Sitko smirked. The One Horn Priests were preposterous, though they seemed to take themselves very seriously.

He turned toward the priests and asked, "What kind of costume is that? What are you supposed to be?"

They did not grasp his sarcasm.

"Costume?" one asked, the corners of his rouged mouth twitching as he looked for advice to the other priest, who grimaced as if deaf and dumb.

"Ah," Sitko sighed with an expression of disdain, "apparently you are not prepared to answer questions."

Once again the One Horn Priests bowed ceremoniously, and then they gestured toward the door, indicating that they wanted Sitko to lead the way out of the prison. He nodded in agreement but he did not move. He brushed off his filthy clothes, which had not been washed during all his time of captivity. And then, slowly and deliberately, he walked to the door.

As he approached the priests they tried to take him by the arms, but Sitko pulled away. "Wait! I am not an invalid." But they ignored his objections and quickly took hold of him with a methodical, practiced, and tight grip.

Sitko walked rigidly between them, their three bodies interlocked so tightly that they merged with one another. As they came out into the evening, Sitko tried to see the priests more clearly than had been possible in the dusk of his prison.

He was repelled by their theatrics. By their coy pretense of seriousness. By their vacant little eyes that tried to convey malice but were only capable of conveying ignorance.

When Sitko realized how impotent his captors were, he

suddenly stopped, and consequently the priests also had to stop.

"Why did they send you two, of all people?" he exclaimed, outraged that his execution was becoming a charade.

They responded with artificial expressions of solemnity, but they did not speak, either having no answer or having no idea what Sitko was talking about.

"I will go no farther!" Sitko said, uncertain how the priests would react.

No answer was needed. The One Horn Priests refused to loosen their grip, and they began to push Sitko forward, though he tried to resist.

"What difference does it make what you do?" he shouted. "You're going to kill me anyway! So I might as well get the satisfaction of spitting in your faces!"

As he struggled in vain against them, he thought of flies struggling to free themselves from flypaper until their legs were torn off. Somehow the idea made him laugh with disgust.

"You will not find it easy to snuff me out!" he shouted defiantly. "I do not intend to go quietly! If it is something ridiculous that you want, I'll give you something ridiculous!"

After a moment, Sitko realized the futility of resistance. There was no point in being heroic. There was no purpose in snatching at life. And so he moved forward, and their entangled bodies faltered and stumbled across the plaza. He was their prisoner, but they allowed him to lead the way, though he had no idea where he was going.

They left the plaza and passed over a bridge constructed of rough planks, crossing a ditch still swollen by runoff from the cloudburst. The water glistened and trembled in the moon-light. They passed near several dilapidated adobe houses and down a succession of ruined lanes where dogs and raccoons sniffed piles of garbage.

As they turned a corner into an open field, a young man with a rusty saber approached them. Sitko lurched and forci-bly pulled the One Horn Priests forward, gradually breaking into a run, and his two companions, puffing and panting, had to run beside him.

Now they left the village behind, moving out into the open desert. Eventually they reached a small stone quarry, deserted and ransacked. Here the One Horn Priests came to a halt, either because this was their destination or because they were simply too exhausted to go any farther.

At last they loosened their grip on Sitko, who stood idly while the priests wiped their brows and adjusted their head-dresses, which had turned lopsided during the journey.

The Moon shone down on everything with a sharpness and coldness that no other light possesses. Sitko looked up at the Moon, but he was no longer frightened—not by the Moon and not by the One Horn Priests.

After an exchange of formalities regarding which of them was to take charge of the next task, one of the priests came up to Sitko and removed his shirt and pants in a set of rehearsed actions. Sitko shivered, and the priest gave him a reassuring pat on the shoulder, while the other man carefully folded Sitko's clothes as if they would be used again.

Then the priest took Sitko by the arm and led him back and forth, as if to keep him warm, while the other man surveyed the quarry to find a suitable spot.

Sitko was led to a place near the rock face where a large

smooth boulder was lying. The two priests ceremoniously laid Sitko down on the ground, propping him against the boulder, and placed his head on the rock.

Despite all their pains his position remained awkward. So one of the priests urged the other to allow him to deal with Sitko by himself. But his efforts resulted in little improvement. Every time he rearranged Sitko's position on the ground he ended up with the same grotesque results. Finally the One Horn Priests sighed in dismay and gave up.

Slowly, one of the priests opened a narrow sheath that was suspended from his waistband and drew out a long, thin, double-edged knife, holding it up and testing the cutting edges in the moonlight. Then an elaborate but clumsy ceremony began. One priest handed the knife across Sitko's chest to the other, who handed it back again. The ritual was repeated again and again. Sitko could see no purpose in it. Perhaps they could not decide which priest should be the one to use the knife. Perhaps they had no intention of killing him. Or maybe they wanted to provoke Sitko into grabbing the knife himself as it went back and forth from hand to hand above him and plunging it into his own heart. But he refused to do so. He merely turned away and gazed around him, ignoring the movement of the knife, back and forth above his chest.

His glance fell on the top story of a little house near the quarry. With a flicker, as if a candle were being lighted, a window suddenly opened. A human figure, faint and insubstantial at that distance, leaned abruptly far forward and stretched both arms still farther. Sitko was entranced by the image. *Who was it? A friend? A good man? Someone who sympathized? Someone who wanted to help? Was it one person only? Or were they all there? All the people of his life? Was there still a chance for him? Were there arguments in his favor that had been overlooked?*

Of course there must be! Hatred was unshakable, but it could not destroy a person who wanted to go on living.

He raised his hands and spread out all his fingers. Then he shouted and leaped to his feet.

The One Horn Priests were completely unprepared for his defiance. They fell back and the knife tumbled to the ground.

"Enough!" Sitko shouted, standing naked in the cold desert air and shivering. Then the One Horn Priests locked him in their tight grip and hurried with him back to the prison.

SIXTEEN

Because I could not stop for Death
He kindly stopped for me.
The Carriage held but just Ourselves—
And Immortality.

—E<small>MILY</small> D<small>ICKINSON</small>

T<small>HE RAIN HAD</small> washed the dirt floor clean. There was no evidence of the flood except a faint water stain high upon the whitewashed walls. No sooner had the deluge come than it vanished without a trace, leaving the desert as barren as it was before the storm. The soil was slick and dry and hard. The night was exceptionally cool. A mockingbird filled the air with its endless trills. And crickets resounded from everywhere in the moonless night, making a needle-work of melody.

Sitko sat hunched on the ground near the little fire in the center of the room. He was spreading a thick black coat of charcoal upon the remaining piece of cardboard, concentrating on nothing but his work lest he panic at the thought that at any moment the One Horn Priests would return to finish him off.

No matter how he tried to focus his mind on nothing but

his picture, an insidious panic overtook him, and random, bitter words flew like shrapnel through his dark thoughts. He was as disgusted with himself as he was with his captors. They were driven by stupidity and arrogance, intent upon no purpose but finding an excuse to destroy him. Clinging to any justification, any falsehood, no matter how unlikely or absurd. Blind to all arguments except their own. And he himself was no better. Instead of laughing in their faces, instead of standing up to them or fighting them, he had quietly accepted their rules. He had done absolutely nothing to escape or to defend himself. Out of fear of himself. Out of self-contempt. Driven by fear. Driven by a belief in their hatred. And now it was too late!

He groaned with anger as he smeared the surface of the cardboard with yet another deep black coating, covering it entirely, leaving not the slightest trace of open space. No light. No air. No exit.

Just as he was finishing the picture, he heard angry voices at the door of his prison. In a moment, the door was flung open and Patu rushed into the room, looking perturbed and anxious, as if the One Horn Priests had tried to keep her from entering the prison.

Sitko greeted her with an exhausted and ironic chortle. "So now they don't want you to visit me!" he muttered. "They want me all to themselves, do they?" he exclaimed as Patu squatted on the floor, her eyes filled with exasperation. "Isn't that typical!" Sitko shouted so the One Horn Priests could hear him. "The defenders of the people turn out to be impostors."

"Do not think of them," Patu said with great effort, as if she were holding back a flood of emotion. "I have sent them away. They will not return till morning."

Then suddenly she sobbed.

Sitko hurried to his friend's side. "What have they done to you?" he asked with concern.

Patu shook her head as she wiped away her tears.

"Patu, tell me what they have done to you!"

"They have done nothing," she whispered. "They have done nothing to me. I am a powerful woman. The people of this village love me. They will not harm me!"

"But why are you crying? What is the matter?"

Patu hushed Sitko and made a wide gesture. "Listen," she whispered. "Listen and you will know why I weep. Listen! What do you hear?"

Sitko held his breath and listened intently.

"What do you mean?" he asked. "I hear mockingbirds and crickets."

"Yes, that is all you hear. . . ."

Again Sitko listened for some unfamiliar sound in the night. But there was nothing.

"There is one thing you do not hear that you have heard every night that you have been in our village," Patu murmured sadly. "You do not hear the voices of the children. You do not hear them."

"Oh, my God!" Sitko cried. "Patu, you must tell me! What has happened here? What has happened to the children?"

Patu sobbed as she fell to the ground.

Sitko embraced her, drawing her into his lap and rocking back and forth as tears came into his eyes. "I'm so sorry . . ." Sitko whispered as he tried to comfort her. "Please believe me . . . I am not responsible for this! I am not an evil person. Please do not do believe that I made such a thing happen!"

"Now it does not matter who is to blame . . ." she wept. "Now it does not matter who the evil one is. For me, it does not matter anymore. But for the children . . . aih, for the little children it matters."

An immense rage overtook Sitko. He roared as he leaped to his feet. "My God! What kind of people are these? What kind of people live in this village? How could they do this?"

"It is the One Horn Priests," Patu said with a great sigh, as she laboriously sat up and leaned against the wall, gazing into Sitko's face. "They were shamed for their failure. Delito told them to kill you, but they did not know how to kill you. They fought with one another. They argued over which of them would do it. That is what happened. And they failed. And so Delito shamed them in the meeting chamber, in front of all the elders. He took away their pride. He took away their power. And so they wanted to fight with everyone. They wanted to show a strength they do not have. And what did they do? They went into the underground chamber where the children were kept and they butchered them! They stabbed them and they killed them and they cut off their arms and their legs and their heads! Their blood is everywhere. The walls are covered with their blood!"

"But why? Why did they do such a thing?"

Patu opened her mouth and threw back her head with a long, fierce cry. Then she sat in silence for a long time, staring at the ground. After a long time she mumbled distractedly: "Why . . . why do we do it? Aih," she groaned, looking intently at Sitko. "We do it because that is the way it is for us. That is why. You do not understand. Perhaps I do not understand. But that is the way it must be. No one can change these things. They are written in our hearts, from the first day of our lives. These things are what we are. And without them we are nothing."

Sitko slowly shook his head in disbelief. "No . . ." he murmured, "I refuse to listen to you. That cannot be true. There are many ways to live, but a people who can do what has been done here . . . such a people know nothing about life. What they know is death. I cannot accept that. You are my friend, but I cannot accept what you say. I cry out against such a vision of life. You have been kind to me and I have listened to the things you believe, but I can feel nothing but horror for the things that have happened here."

A mockingbird filled the air with his endless lament. Crickets called from everywhere in the moonless night. Sitko and Patu sat silently listening to the dark songs. Then Sitko put some sticks on the little fire. He glanced down at the picture he was making, studying it momentarily, and then he pushed it away in disgust. He groaned as he saw the blackness of his picture, an image without a trace of air or sky.

Patu picked up the cardboard and nodded sadly as she looked at the lightless world Sitko had painted. "It is as dark as night," she said. "A night without stars. It is the longest night. And in the morning, Delito has told them to tie your hands and feet. And then he will come to this room. And he himself will kill you. Like a dog. That is what he will do. And there is nothing I can do to stop him."

Sitko looked at her with an expression of overwhelming exhaustion. Then he nodded dejectedly. "And is this the way it ends?"

"How would you have it end?" Patu quietly asked, a drawn and tired look on her face.

Sitko shrugged with resignation. "What did I hope for? Did I think I would win the love of the world? Probably. That's probably what I believed. I guess I took it for granted that everything would be okay. I didn't think that it would end like this. I wanted *something* from life. I hoped that in the end everything would begin to make sense. But it doesn't make sense. That isn't the way it is. So how does a person live a life? And how does a person die? I really don't know. Perhaps you know these things, my friend, but I know nothing about them. Did I think that there would be some happy times? Yes, of course, I thought I would be happy at long last. But happiness passes so quickly that I have difficulty recalling it. We must imagine ourselves to be happy. What we remember is pain. We always remember pain, but we rarely recall its purpose. What we remember is the long hard dying of life. What we remember is the terrible indignities of living. The horror of it. The absurdity of it. The unspeakable monstrousness of it. That is what we remember. And when we remember it, we are afraid."

"This thing that frightens you, my friend, it is called death," Patu said quietly with a serene expression in her dark eyes. "We hide from it like children, and we think it doesn't see us. So we do not worry about it. But we do not have to think about it, because it thinks about us. One day it will take our lives into its palm and blow them out. And that will be the end of you and me. When I look across the desert and beyond the mountains that are the rim of the world, when I search for the faces of my friends who are gone, I cannot help thinking about the day when everything must die and all that has been can be no more. I sometimes sit here under a storm of stars watching them burn their separate fires in the enormous sky. And always as I watch something happens. Look . . . far out in the darkness . . . and you will see it too. There! A star dies! Did you see? There is not a night when some great star does not fall from the sky. One day even our great father the Sun will fall. Because all the stars are fathers and all must die. I do not understand it, my friend. I do not try. I only know that there is a thing called death, and we cannot know how good it is to be alive until we have seen the stars . . . the birds . . . our fathers . . . fall."

"You make everything sound terrible," Sitko exclaimed, going to the window and searching the black sky for some sign of light. "If that is all there is to life, it's a wonder you want to live."

For a moment Patu smiled rather sadly. Then she nodded slowly and said: "No, Sitko Ghost Horse, the wonder is that we have lived at all."

With her words, all at once, a nightborne fragrance flew through the window, filling the little room. It swept passed them in dense waves, floating heavily in the air, balmy and intoxicating, like an embrace. The scent astonished Sitko. The little fire in the center of the room suddenly went out, leaving them in utter darkness. The night was filled with a cascade of mockingbird warbles and the pulsing singing of crickets.

Sitko did not realize that he was weeping until he felt tears running down his cheeks. He opened his eyes and found himself in that place at the center where the light and all it remembers is born out of the mouth of darkness. He gasped for breath, like a swimmer emerging from a deep stream. And he sighed as he saw the faint outline of Patu's body, black against black, a massive shape that shined dimly in the dark.

"Now I must say farewell to you, Sitko Ghost Horse. Soon the Sun comes. And soon it will be over. I have done what I could do. There is nothing more for me. So I must say farewell."

Sitko did not respond.

"I will remember you," Patu whispered.

"When you look at the picture I gave you, please think of me."

"I will think of you, Sitko Ghost Horse, but I do not have the picture, for they came and took it away and burned it."

"You must have something from me," Sitko said, holding up the cardboard he had covered with charcoal. "I will finish this picture and leave it here on the ledge for you."

Patu did not speak. In the darkness Sitko saw her figure lean mournfully forward. He could hear her breathing but he could not see her. He stared into the lightless room, trying to glimpse the face of the extraordinary person who had become his friend. But he could see nothing but the dim radiance surrounding her body.

Then abruptly Patu got up, hobbled to the door, and disappeared.

For a moment, there was silence. Then a breeze flew past, swiftly rising as it carried the night's sweet scent. Suddenly, the little fire in the center of the room ignited, lighting the room. The crackle of the flames awakened the sounds of the world, and the voice of the mockingbirds and the chirping of crickets resounded everywhere.

Soon it would be dawn and they would be coming for him. There was no time left. It was over. With great effort he dismissed his somber thoughts and quickly found the cardboard and put it on the ledge so he could examine it. The surface was shadowed by a dense blackness. It was just as he had imagined it. Black. Blank. Meaningless. It was the image he wanted to leave behind.

Covering his fingers with the powdered embers at the cold edges of the fire, he rubbed the black surface of the picture, intensifying its depth and darkness. And then he was done. He studied the picture and nodded with satisfaction. It was the end. It was finished now. And yet, he could not keep his fingers still. The picture beckoned to them. And when they returned to the surface of the cardboard, they rapidly moved across the surface. With a bit of bright white chalk he shattered the darkness of the picture, drawing a gleaming bolt of lightning that zigzagged across the lightless picture like a heartline, plunging through the bleak surface and bursting outward into a space as immense and unbounded and luminous as the trail of the wind.

Sitko Ghost Horse drew in the breath of life, and he wept.

That great clean gust of air filled him with infinite sorrow and regret. In the wind came the long lonely songs of the dead stretching endlessly behind him. He sat alone, holding the picture in his hands, staring into the emptiness of the shadows that came with the dawn. Nothing moved. Nothing was born and nothing grew. There was only the long lean torment of a deathly gale full of dead voices.

Then from a distance came a small sound. Somehow it was familiar, but he could not identify it. It came from far away and from long ago. Sitko stirred, and his face filled with excitement. But the sound faded and the tears came back into his eyes.

He quickly glanced around, sensing that someone was approaching. How could he resist? How could he fight against them without weapons?

He leaped to his feet, ready to fight them off, ready to battle anyone who entered the door.

It was at that moment that he noticed it.

The door.

It was open.

His heart pounded. He held his breath and cautiously approached the doorway. He peered around the corner and out into the village. The desert was filled with a terrible silence. It was utterly dark except for the fragile ribbon of dawn that lay along the crest of the distant mountains.

Then, slowly, from behind a great black cloud, the Moon came into the pitiless sky. Dust twisted aimlessly over the forlorn earth. In the moonlight he searched everywhere for a sign of people. No one was in sight.

Sitko ducked back into the room, for fear that someone might see him and realize that the door of his prison had been left open. He tried to catch his breath, but he was so excited that he trembled with expectation. He searched the room for something he could use to defend himself, but there was only the piece of cardboard with the picture of a streak of lightning shattering the darkness. He snatched it and held it in both hands like a shield. And then he carefully reapproached the door and, covering himself with the picture, he stood in the opening, gazing with disbelief at the immense open space that surrounded him.

There was no one out there. No one. He carefully moved a bit forward to see if someone might be watching him. To see if all of this was just an elaborate trick.

No one stirred.

Now he was overcome with excitement and relief. He could escape! This time he could be free.

He darted back into the room and laid the picture on the ledge where he had promised to leave it. Then he walked slowly through the open door and into the moonlight.

As he hurried toward the mountains, he did not notice the sweet odor of decay that followed after him. He did not see the obedient shadows trailing doggedly in his footsteps, nor the trail of cinders and blood that left its terrible blemish upon the earth. He searched into the openness of the sky, filled with an exceptional delight. But he was unaware of the long, twisted shadow of a man that slipped out of the darkness and silently followed after him. All he could see was the vast freedom of the land. His bare feet stung on the hard ground, but he began to chuckle softly, unable to restrain himself. He was free! He was free to listen to music, to eat, and to paint!

The thought of life brought the memory of all the love that had vanished with the precious people he had known. And the joy of life that filled him collided with the sad memories of the dead.

He began to run headlong across the vast and empty landscape, and he cried out for a sign that the good days had not gone away forever. He begged the sky for a sign that he would survive, that he might once again raise himself with the vision that had been given to him so many years ago.

Then there was that same familiar sound in the distance. Again, the distant sound!

Sitko stopped abruptly and listened. For a moment it seemed as if that noise in the silent world had evaded him. But then, he heard it once again, and he wept as he recognized the small song that crept feebly from the throat of the earth.

"I am your vision," it said. *"I am the seed that grows. I am the cave of your heart and the drum that summons legends and dreams!"*

"Aih!" Sitko exclaimed, as he opened his arms to the night and began to run, leaving a trail of colors behind him. With a shout of delight he dove into the deep darkness that stretched beneath the vast beadwork of the sky.

Far out in the desert, beyond the brown grass and the dead trees, a bright red creature ran into the stars.

It was a fox! Sniffing the dark land where the ceremonial fire still burned and where tiny shadows were cast against a gigantic sea of human dream and memory.

"Yes . . ." Sitko murmured with a gentle smile as he ran into the deepest night. "It is a fox!"

▲

*"The path of the mythological adventure is a rite of passage:
Departure, Initiation, and Return. The hero ventures forth
from the world of common day into a region of supernatural forces
where he penetrates the source of some mysterious power,
and, finally, he makes his life-enhancing return to the world."*

JOSEPH CAMPBELL, *Hero With a Thousand Faces*

▼